C000157699

THE RELUCTANT ADVENTURES

OF

FLETCHER CONNOLLY

ON THE

INTERSTELLAR RAILROAD

VOLUME 4

SUPERMASSIVE BLACKGUARD

F. R. SAVAGE

THE RELUCTANT ADVENTURES OF FLETCHER CONNOLLY ON THE INTERSTELLAR RAILROAD VOLUME 4 SUPERMASSIVE BLACKGUARD

Copyright © 2016 by Felix R. Savage

The right to be identified as the author of this work has been asserted by Felix R. Savage. All rights reserved. No part of this book may be reproduced in any form or by any electronic or mechanical means, including information storage and retrieval systems, without written permission from the publisher or author.

First published in the United States of America in 2016 by Knights Hill Publishing.

Cover art by Christian Bentulan
Interior design and layout by Felix R. Savage

ISBN-10: 1-937396-23-1
ISBN-13: 978-1-937396-23-7

THE RELUCTANT ADVENTURES

OF

FLETCHER CONNOLLY

ON THE

INTERSTELLAR RAILROAD

VOLUME 4

SUPERMASSIVE BLACKGUARD

CHAPTER 1

Everyone says you should stay well away from the Ghost Train. I thought a couple of hundred miles would be far enough. But the bloody thing's got some kind of monstrous invisible effector field. Our ship is trapped, and we're being sucked inexorably towards the train.

It's the size of several oil tankers joined end to end, clamped onto the Interstellar Railroad with a thousand chain dogs, like a silver caterpillar on an infinitely long twig. I stare at the fractal steel tangle of its undercarriage. Sparks of unholy coloration and lurid intensity wriggle in there.

Well. We would probably have been shot dead the moment we set foot on Treetop, anyway. We're in a stolen police cruiser, *and* I've got a stolen A-tech artefact worth billions stuck down my swimming togs.

I had to stuff it in there to have my hands free for my lightsaber. As if there's any way I could possibly fight this.

The wall of the Ghost Train fades like mist, and we drift helplessly inside.

It looks like a vast parking lot. This is the end carriage of the Ghost Train, the boxcar I suppose, and it's huge, as long as two football fields. We're still under the control of the mysterious force that sucked us in here. Imogen, my partner in crime, is sitting in the driver's seat, but she's obviously not piloting the cruiser. She's got her hands clamped over her face and she's crying quietly.

I pat her shoulder. She shakes my hand off.

I gaze out of the window. The floor is packed solid with vehicles ranging from Silicon People gravsleds to *bicycles*, fact o' God, and several classical-style flying saucers.

We land as lightly as a feather in a parking space exactly the right size for the police cruiser.

For a moment we all sit in silence.

Breathe, Fletch. *Breathe.*

We're not the first people to board the Ghost Train in the forty-odd years since humanity began to explore the Interstellar Railroad. The Ghost Train makes a circuit of the galaxy every two years, you see. No one knows where it comes from, or who built it. There are these automated maintenance entities that came with the Railroad—we call them gandy dancers, and maybe they know something about the Ghost Train, but they aren't talking. It is thought they *can't* talk.

What we do know is that not one of the poor souls who've boarded the Ghost Train in the past has ever returned.

I try to recall if we're the first ever to board the Ghost Train *by accident.*

There are four of us. Myself and Imogen, and then there's Sam, who helped us rob the King of Treetop. He's the son of a notorious female pirate who's currently in jail on Earth. The fourth member of our unwilling crew is my uncle Finian Connolly. He used to be a pirate, too. Now he's a sherriff in the Near Earth Police Department. The police cruiser is his. We took it without his permission, needless to say. He's a bloodthirsty old bastard.

Now he's crouched behind the cockpit, looking haggard and afraid, pulling on one end of his white moustache.

Imogen breaks the silence, mumbling, "Our Father who art in heaven …" I never knew she was a believer. I'm a Catholic myself. Save us from the fires of hell, and the trains of long-dead aliens.

I take a deep breath, lean across Imogen, and peer at the exterior sensor readout. It says the parking lot is pressurized at exactly one Earth atmosphere.

Here goes nothing. I release the pressure seals.

My ears pop.

A grin spreads across my face.

"Right, we're not dead yet. That's something."

I open my door. It crunches into the side of the vehicle next to us. Squeezing out, I see that this vehicle is a Denebite star shuttle. Its shovel-nose juts over the aisle in front of the police cruiser. Jesus, no one's *ever* found an undamaged one!

And on the other side of the cruiser is a Sagittarian monowheel, like a paddlewheel steamer glued on top of a giant gray duvet. Its decorative horns claw towards the bright white lights in the ceiling. The Sagittarians were great ones for putting horns on everything.

My grin gets wider. The old excitement is tickling at my brain. The thrill of the A-tech hunt. The elation of discovery. It's like adrenaline, you know, what the ancient Celts called the berserker madness. It can keep you going when any rational man would be curled up weeping in a corner.

There's music playing.

Patsy Cline, actually. *I Fall to Pieces*.

My grin gets a bit strained, but I urge Imogen out of the cruiser. "Come on love, on your feet."

Finian squeezes out of the rear passenger-side door—it's the only one that will open all the way. He stares around, mentally valuing everything we see, if I know him. He may have put on an NEPD uniform, and shaved off the Old Testament beard he used to sport, but he hasn't changed that much.

Sam is ahead of us all. He's already halfway up the side of the star shuttle. It's not quite undamaged. Holes in the hull, which appear to have been punched out by large slugs, make handy footholds. Sam balances twenty feet up, peering into the portholes.

"There are skeletons in there," he says, pop-eyed.

Well, that's grand news. I force a confident tone. "There could be other stuff around the place. It's huge. Let's explore properly."

Imogen sinks down on her heels with a sigh, propping her back against the cruiser's hubcap and wrapping her arms around her knees.

"Well, I am an A-tech scout," I say, spreading my arms. I used to be, anyway, before I turned to crime.

"Talking of A-tech," Finian says, showing his yellow snaggleteeth. "Did youse see those flying saucers? I'm going to have a look at those."

I grit my teeth, watching him stroll off. Nothing about the wisdom, or unwisdom, of splitting up in a place like this. Not even a see you later.

"Ah well." I turn to Sam. "Let's go this way."

"No, let's go towards the back of the train."

"This is towards the back of the train, idjit."

We argue pointlessly about this for a few minutes and then set off in the arbitrary direction I chose, as opposed to the arbitary direction Sam chose. At least it made Imogen laugh, although her laughter dies very quickly behind us. She said she would lock herself in the police cruiser until we return.

My steps echo on the deck, which seems to be made of corrugated iron, except it can't be or it'd have rusted. Sam's footsteps angle off to my right.

I walk between spaceships from every galactic civilization known to man, and some I cannot place at all. All the aliens are dead, and have been for millions or billions of years. Each species in its turn flourished, expanded, colonized, and then ran into another species that finished it off, or else obliterated itself through some combination of stupidity and planet-busting weapons. Humanity is now the only sapient species in the galaxy. We have found plenty of A-tech in our explorations, and thousands of people have got rich reverse-engineering it, but everything we find is old, old, old.

In contrast, these ships look as if they were just parked in here yesterday. No dust, no rust. I bang a fist on the side of a Puzzler space chariot, and the metal gives back a solid boom.

"What was that?" Sam shouts, from somewhere far away on my right.

"Just me," I shout back.

I keep walking. And all the time, country music keeps playing from somewhere up ahead of me. Now Willie Nelson is *On the Road Again.* Quite apt. The volume is meager, the sound quality's shite, and I would very much like to know why *and how* the aliens who built the Ghost Train got to know about 20th century American country music. Time travel? Oh Jesus, no. Please.

There *has* to be a rational explanation for this.

CHAPTER 2

The country music is coming from somewhere ahead of me.

Following the sound, I enter a jam-packed area of the parking bay. Fitted in around the spaceships, in such numbers that only narrow aisles are left open to walk through, are bicycles, motorcycles, sleighs, gondolas, monowheels, cars, and other vehicles so weird I can only guess what kind of terrain they once travelled over. My interior trainspotter gets overwhelmed by the sheer variety. In some places there are solid walls of A-tech rising up on either side of my head. It's as if someone amused themselves by fitting all the things together like 3D jigsaws.

There were *bones* in that star shuttle Sam investigated ... I shudder, and walk faster.

I hope it was not a very bad idea to split up.

I'm carrying my lightsaber in my right hand. It's a brilliant weapon, and the powerpack is still at least half charged, but I don't think it would be very much use against whoever it was that could kidnap Denebites.

The walls get lower. Now there's only one layer of vehicles on the deck.

Further down the long, straight aisle I'm in, I spot the rear end of a pickup truck sticking out of its parking space.

It's a Dodge Ram.

They still make those. But this isn't the new, anti-grav-equipped, flying model. It's the *old* kind of pickup truck, that only ran on roads.

The music is definitely coming from the Dodge.

I amble closer and marvel at the truck's bumper stickers.

Keep Texas Armed.

Buchanan For President.

Dallas Cowboys 1992 Super Bowl Champions.

The pickup is parked on a corner. Another aisle crosses this one beyond it. I walk around the pickup, and bellow in shock.

There's a man in the cab!

He's sat with his boots up on the dashboard, an acoustic guitar on his lap. Sixtyish, gray-haired, as lean as a strip of beef jerky, he's playing—and singing, tunelessly—along with Willie Nelson.

He sees me at the same time I see him.

The boots go down, the guitar goes on the passenger seat, and a 1911-style handgun pops out of a holster I didn't see before.

I instinctively duck.

BLAM! He fires a round into the Sagittarian amphibious tricycle on the other side of the aisle I'm in.

I sprint back the way I came. As I skid around the corner, another round smashes into the electric purple articulated halftrack beyond me, so close I practically get a friction burn on my scalp.

If I stay in this long straight aisle, it'll be like a shooting gallery for him. I leap on top of a Pygmy Ent tractor, and plunge down the other side on top of a heap of scooters. They clank, settling under my weight.

The door of the Dodge Ram slams. The man's footsteps thud down the aisle. "Where ya at, asshole?"

Should I stay put, or keep moving? I'm in a narrow crevice. I can see where I might be able to wriggle under a Silicon People gravsled. I shift my weight. The scooters rattle again. I freeze.

"I heard that! Where ya hiding? Come out and show yourself!" His voice approaches my hiding place. "You ain't got no reason to be scared. This is the safest place in the galaxy. HA!"

BLAM! He fires another round into the Pygmy Ent tractor.

I nearly piss myself in terror. But he hasn't seen me, after all. That was just Texan punctuation.

His footsteps move past. Maybe I should pop up and stab him in the back with my lightsaber. *If* he doesn't hear me moving, and shoot first.

"Oh, here's a good one! I like this one."

Willie Nelson has turned over the mic to Johnny Cash, and now this Texan lunatic begins to sing along. "An old cowboy went ridin' out one dark and windy day, upon a ridge he rested—" *BLAM!* "I see you! *There* you are! I got you covered!"

Trying not to make any more noise, I twist from the waist. Oh Jesus, there's Sam, up on top of a spaceship with a melted-looking hole in its side. He's lying flat between two bulges on the nose of the ship.

BLAM! One of the bulges shatters. Sam jerks back from

the shrapnel.

"Screw y'all," grits the Texan. From the pause, I gather he's reloading.

Johnny Cash sings on, and without thinking about it, I start to sing with him:

As the riders loped on by him, he heard one call his name
'If you wanna save your soul from hell, ridin' on our range
Then cowboy, change your ways today, or with us you will ride
Tryin' to catch the devil's herd across these endless skies ...'

Johnny Cash was an Irishman, you know.

"Huh?" screeches the Texan. "Who's that singin'?"

I lean back against the Pygmy Ent tractor and give him the chorus. I could never be a singer by profession, I like money too much, but I've got a decent voice. I used to do the vocals when my friend Donal would play his fiddle for ceili nights on the *Skint Idjit*. We'd have the girls weeping at *Spancil Hill* and *Missing You,* never mind they'd never been within a thousand miles of Ireland. Everyone on the Railroad can relate to a song about being far from home.

And apparently the Texan feels the same way about Johnny Cash's musical parable. His face pokes over the top of the Pygmy Ent tractor. There's a twisted smile on his lips. "Hey man." He sits up on the tractor and beats out the rhythm on its roof. We finish out the song. I bow, as best I can, and he claps. "You got a good set of pipes."

"I heard you playing the guitar. You're not bad yourself."

"Oh hell, I got nothing else to do 'sides practice. We should have a session sometime."

"Can you give me a hand up at all?"

"You stuck?" the Texan chuckles. "Sure." He helps me out with a dry, guitar-callused grip that turns into a handshake when we're both stood on top of the Pgymy Ent tractor. "Caleb Dunhill. Pleased to meetcha. I'm from Roswell, Texas."

"Fletcher Connolly, from Lisdoonvarna, County Clare." I glance down at his 1911, now back in its holster. "Any particular reason you were trying to blow my head off?"

"Aw, man, I 'pologize for that. I thought you were an alien."

I glance up at the spaceship. Sam is swarming down its side. "That's my friend Sam, from the Omega Centauri Cluster. He's *not* an alien," I add, just in case Caleb gets the wrong idea.

Caleb looks me up and down. He's not looking at the lightsaber in my right hand. When it's switched off, it just looks like a short stick with alien writing on it. He's looking at my clothes. Or rather, the lack of them. "That what they usually wear in County Clare?"

I am wearing a pair of Speedos, black work shoes, and nothing else. My shirt got left behind at a holiday resort on Treetop's moon, and my trousers got covered with blood during the same episode. They were too disgusting to put on again. Mercifully, it's not cold in here.

"It's a long story," I say. "But no, this is not how I normally dress, and I'd be very grateful if there might be some clothes around here I could borrow." That don't come off dead aliens. I decide against adding that. I don't want to get him started thinking about aliens again.

"There might be," he says. "You been on board long?"

"We have not. We just got here. You?"

Caleb cackles. "Longer than you been alive, I bet. What year is it now?"

"2067."

"Lord, how the time flies. I was abducted in 1994. Whatcha think of that?"

I don't believe him. He appears to be about sixty, spry and leathery, with cowlicks in his silver-gray hair. On the other hand … those bumper stickers.

"I'd say you've not missed much," I tell him. "The twenty-first century was an awful shambles until the Railroad came along. Since then, it's been teeth and nails and devil take the hindmost. Everyone's racing to find the best A-tech and make money off it. On the bright side, there are no wars anymore, because everyone's busy getting rich."

"That's what I heard from the last guy came through here. He told me about the Railroad, how every man with an ounce of smarts and a pound of motivation can make his fortune. Better 'n the Texas oil rush!"

If it was that easy, I would be king of my own planet by now. "Your man may have painted it a bit too rosy."

Sam reaches us in time to hear the last part. "What's the Texas oil rush?" he says.

Caleb eyes him. Sam is also wearing Speedos and nothing else, for the same reasons as me. He hasn't even got shoes on. "Your friend said you was from the Omega Centauri cluster?"

"Uh uh," Sam says. "I lived there when I was in my teens. But I was born on Cygnus 2c. My mom was into truffalo farming back then. Second worst mistake of her life. Number one was my dad."

"Okayyy," says Caleb.

I cough. "This fella who told you about the Railroad. Is he still around?"

Caleb doesn't seem to hear me. "Say." His eyes brighten. "Did they impeach Clinton?"

"Oh, Jesus." I know which Clinton he's talking about, a 20th-century US president. But history was never my best class in school, when I was in school, which was not often. I prefer to think of myself as an autodidact. Strangely enough, US presidents have never been very high on my list of things to Google. "Sorry. I don't know. Maybe not? It was before I was born."

Caleb sighs. "I been waiting seventy years to find out if they nailed that son-of-a-bitch."

"They're all sons of bitches," Sam says.

"Ain't that the truth."

"That's why the Railroad is so great. You can get away from the politicians," says this son of a pirate who styled herself the empress of the Omega Centauri galactic cluster. "But guess what? They've set up a police force in space now. It's called the Near Earth Police Department, woop woop. It's the beginning of the end."

"Shee-it. Is there anything the government can't ruin?"

"Fletch! Sam! FLETCHER!"

Finian must be a fair distance away, but he's got brass lungs on him. Johnny Cash can't compete.

"We've—FOUND—the—WAY—OUT!"

CHAPTER 3

"No, he ain't found the way out," Caleb says. "There is no way out."

This gives me pause. After all, Caleb should know.

But hope resists reason. I jog towards Finian's voice. Sam's already taken off running. Caleb ambles after us, in no hurry.

"OVER—HERE!" Finian shouts.

Breathless, I catch up with Sam. We round a corner and there's Finian. Imogen is with him.

She's holding a fistful of Finian's sleeve, cowering behind him.

I can see why.

"This is Dizzy and this is Pew Pew," says Finian, beaming.

Dizzy and Pew Pew are gandy dancers.

They are sitting in lawn chairs at a folding table beside the steps of an honest-to-God supermarket tabloid UFO. Their stubby three-fingered hands hold playing cards. It looks as if they were in the middle of a game of Beggar My Neighbor. The cards are dogeared and fluffy around the edges. Dizzy wears a homburg and Pew Pew a fedora, and both are clad in overalls, which look like pantomime costumes on them, since they are *gandy dancers.*.

Gandy dancers are the maintenance entities that came with the Interstellar Railroad. They have bulgy foreheads, big black eyes that are totally devoid of expression, and little mouths like goldfish. It is thought they are not actually alive, because they don't do the things that civilized sophonts do, such as conquering planets, fighting over them, reducing them to rubble, picking through the rubble for saleable items, etc. Also, they try to be helpful in their way. It is not unheard-of, when a ship comes off the Railroad in deep space, for the gandy dancers to put it back on the tracks, although that's certainly never happened to me, and you can't believe everything you read on the internet.

But Finian's grinning like he has just won the lottery. He clearly thinks the gandy dancers will help us get off the Ghost Train.

"This is Sam, and here's my nephew Fletch," he introduces us.

"I CAN SEE THE RESEMBLANCE," says Pew Pew (fedora).

They *can* talk!

"Jesus, I hope not," Finian chuckles. "Now what was it you were saying about the way out?"

"YES. EXIT IS THIS WAY."

Imagine if your fridge could talk. That is what Pew Pew's voice sounds like.

"OH HELLO CALEB," says Dizzy. He (she? it?) has a more toaster-ish sound to its voice, and I randomly decide it is a she.

Caleb, ambling up, gives the gandy dancers a slovenly salute. "I'll tag along with you," he says to us. "You'll see."

We follow the gandy dancers through the parking lot for the best part of a mile. Along the way, Caleb introduces himself with exaggerated Texan courtesy to Imogen, and hits it off with Finian. This is in the nature of things. Both of them are aged nutters who enjoy shooting at people. I look forward with anticipation to the moment when Caleb finds out Finian is an agent of the hated government, but Finian does not mention it, and I decide not to give the game away, as it might lead to shooting. I suppose his NEPD uniform just looks to Caleb like some weird futuristic fancy dress.

The parking lot ends in a wall. There is an emergency exit door and a sign that shimmers through different combinations of runes before displaying THIS WAY OUT in English.

I could have found this standing on my head.

Finian is chuckling, stroking his moustache nervously. His face falls when we pass through the door into an ordinary stairwell. Of course, this is not the way out of the Ghost Train at all. Only out of the parking lot.

"Were you expecting to step out onto the surface of Earth?" I say, unable to resist needling Finian. "In the middle of a crop circle, maybe?"

"More likely a *stone* circle," he snarls. "These lads have clearly been around since the galaxy was young. It's far from unreasonable to assume they've got teleportation portals and shite. You've not got the vision to see the possibilities, that's your trouble, Fletch. That always has been your trouble."

"NO TELEPORTATION PORTALS, FINIAN," says

Pew Pew. "THAT WOULD VIOLATE LAWS OF PHYS-ICS."

I can't help laughing.

"What's this, then?" Finian says, waving his arms, as we come out of the stairwell into a blindingly white lounge area with backless couches scattered around. "Are we not violating the laws of physics just standing here? The Interstellar Railroad folds time and space. You can travel twenty lightyears and come back in time for dinner, not a whiff of relativistic time dilation anywhere. If that's not violating the laws of physics—"

"NO VIOLATING."

"How not?"

"IS HARD TO EXPLAIN TO BEINGS OF MEDIO-CRE INTELLIGENCE."

I'm weeping tears of laughter by this point, and Sam's in stitches. It's the shook expression on Finian's face, as if he's swallowed a frog. I bet no one has ever called him a 'being of mediocre intelligence' before. Pew Pew just stands there with his head on one side. Butter wouldn't melt.

"Well said," I gurgle, slapping Pew Pew on the shoulder—and immediately draw back. It feels like slapping the bonnet of a car. No, these lads are not flesh and blood. "Don't worry about explaining the science. Just let us know if there are any more nasty surprises coming." I recall the old alien abduction stories, which gained much more credibility after we found out the bulgy-headed 'aliens' were gandy dancers all along. I devoutly hope we're not about to end up on lab tables with alien probes up our arses. "You aren't planning to, erm, examine us, right?"

"NO, FLETCH," says Dizzy, with a straight face, which is

the only expression she's got. "WE DO NOT DO THAT ANYMORE. HUMANITY HAS ALREADY BEEN CLASSIFIED AS SAPIENT."

"That's good to know," I smile.

"IT TOOK SOME TIME."

"Any of y'all hungry?" Caleb calls. He's on the far side of the lounge, pushing white buttons on the white wall. "I'm a get me a chicken sandwich."

The scent of fried food wafts through the lounge, and I realize I'm so hungry I could eat the horse and chase the jockey. My last meal was a bagel from the police cruiser's emergency food stash.

It turns out that the wall can produce any type of consumer item, not only food. I don't believe Caleb when he says this. Then he types in a request for a Johnny Cash album. The wall's hatch opens and there lies a reflective disk with a hole in the middle.

"What's that?"

"It's a CD, of course." Caleb sticks it into his pocket. "I already got this album, but they get scratched up easy."

He chuckles at our blank faces.

"You was saying something about you want clothes?"

The wall has no respect whatsoever for copyrights and trademarks. I get a pair of Carhartts, with multiple cargo pockets for my lightsaber and other stuff, and a Galway United t-shirt. Sam gets Levis and Adidas sneakers. Once she sees our loot, Imogen gets in on the act and requests a baggy flower-print dress and stripy leggings. That is the way she prefers to dress, unfortunately.

"I'm not a taxi driver anymore," she says. "So why should I wear this dumb uniform?"

She hides behind one of the sofas to change, while we order sandwiches, burgers, and drinks.

The food tastes as good as it looks. Munching, we follow the gandy dancers on a tour of the Ghost Train. This means riding a moving sidewalk, like in airports, down a long, long corridor that must run the length of the whole train. Doors hurriedly mark themselves PRIVATE as we approach. I'm not bothered. I don't want to see where they fold time and space. My crisp sandwich is very tasty, although the Pepsi I ordered to go along with it tastes like sweet, flat water.

"They can't do carbonation," Caleb says.

"Ah you're joking. No beer?"

"Not 'less you like it flat. But if you drink spirits, the Johnnie Walker ain't bad."

American whiskey is atrocious. I'll have to see if the wall can do real whisky, without an e. A naggin of Bushmills would really help right now.

Sam slides up beside me. "What do you think was behind the wall?" he mutters.

"A wee alien short order cook with eight arms."

"I bet it was a Duplicator."

He's using the nickname, as found on backers' wishlists, of the nanotech-based duplicator machine discovered some years back on Seventh Heaven. That one coughed up several perfect duplicates of wristwatches, rocks, and a iPad before conking out, never to be successfully repaired. Idjits! If I'd been one of those explorers I'd have dropped a stack of thousand-dollar bills into it, not my fecking wristwatch. Those copies were perfect down to the atomic level. To be fair, they probably did not have a stack of thousand-dollar bills handy. Still.

"It can't be a Duplicator, Sam. Where would it get the things to duplicate?"

"Maybe it has everything in storage."

"Not a chance." I hold up my sandwich. "I'll bet you anything you like that I'm the first person who's ever asked it for a sandwich of white bread, tons of butter, and prawn cocktail Taytos." I take a big bite.

After a minute, Sam says, "You *are* really eating that."

"The pinnacle of Irish cuisine."

"Prawn cocktail flavor?" Finian booms. "Jesus, that's disgusting. Cheese and onion is the only way to go!"

Sam rolls his eyes. "Anyway," he says in an undertone, "maybe it's not a Duplicator, but are you getting my drift here, Fletch? That's just one example. The buyers would cream their pants over basically everything we've seen so far."

"You're forgetting one thing we've seen so far."

"What?"

"*Bones,* Sam." I hate to be the one to douse the fire of avarice in his young eyes, but someone's got to do it. "You saw bones inside that Denebite ship. I saw some while I was looking around, too. Maybe that's what happens to smart-arses who try to kidnap the short order cook." Or maybe it's what happens to everyone who boards the Ghost Train, sooner or later, but there's no point sharing that dismal speculation.

Sam has already thought of it himself, anyway. I can see it in his eyes.

He laughs humorlessly. "I really wish we had the treecats," he says, gesturing at the latest batch of PRIVATE doors we are passing. "*They'd* be able to get in there."

Thinking of the treecats makes me think of Harriet and Donal. Donal is my best friend and Harriet is his girlfriend. They helped us with the robbery on Treetop. I wonder if they know what's happened to us? Does everyone in the galaxy know by now?

Probably not. I can't see King Zuckerberg of Treetop publically admitting that someone tried to steal his Gizmo of Rejuvenation, and almost got away with it—*did* get away with it, actually. The Gizmo is in the cargo pocket on my right leg, and bloody heavy it is too, dragging my Carhartts down from the waistband. The lightsaber in my left cargo pocket balances it out. I've caught Caleb looking speculatively at the lightsaber's outline: with its powerpack swung down, it is sort of the same shape as a gun. Little does he know that I was going to use it on him if I got line-of-sight.

The moving walkway passes through a misty partition and dumps us into a large, dim, circular room lined with screens.

No.

Windows.

Stars sprinkle a small portion of the wraparound view. The rest of it is a still-life maelstrom of chemical reds and greens, veils of color, dark cirrus streaks, and thunderheads with blazing hearts.

"Welcome to the observation deck!" Caleb says. "That's the Eagle Nebula." He strolls to the nearest window and bends his eye to a telescope. "Where you at, baby? ... *There.*" He beckons us. "Have a look at the Stellar Spire. She's breaking up, but she should be good viewing for another thousand years or so. Whoa! Got a bunch of new stars wasn't there last time we came this way. They're formin' from the cold gas of the nebula. Ain't that right, Pew Pew?"

"THAT IS RIGHT, CALEB."

I turn on the gandy dancers. "Are you expecting us to go all the way around the galaxy with you?"

"THAT IS UP TO YOU, FLETCH," says Dizzy, the cheeky little cow.

I am upset. The Eagle Nebula is 7,000 lightyears away from Earth. It would take a fast spaceship three months to get here, and now the whole interstellar mess is splayed across the Ghost Train's windows in spectroscopic 3D color, seemingly close enough to reach out and touch. We've been travelling for a couple of hours *at most* and we've already gone further from Earth than all but a few of the most reckless explorers have ever ventured.

"What do you mean it's up to me, you cheeky bugger? You abducted us. You've already whisked us seven thousand lightyears from our own neighborhood, and *now* you're saying it's up to us if we want to come?"

"WE DO NOT ABDUCT ANYONE."

"The feck you say," Finian joins in. "You abducted us in broad daylight. Or is it you've got a fetish for collecting vehicles, and we just happened to be inside? Jesus! Kidnapped by the vintage car collectors' society of the Milky Way!"

"YOUR VEHICLE IS NOT PARTICULARLY IN-TERESTING."

"And I suppose we're not particularly interesting, either," I say. "Take us home, then!"

"WE RESPECT FREEDOM OF WILL OF SAPIENT BEINGS."

"Oh, right." I am so angry I could put my fist through one of those windows. "Glad we've got that clear."

"YOU HAVE A CHOICE."

"We do," I drawl.

"YES. YOU CAN STAY ON THE TRAIN, OR YOU CAN GET OFF."

Our stunned silence is broken by the sound of Caleb cackling.

CHAPTER 4

"So this is where we can get off, is it?"

"IF YOU LIKE, FLETCH. THIS IS JUST ONE PLANET."

"Yeah, but this is where you'd recommend?"

Dizzy pauses. "I WOULD NOT LIKE TO STAY HERE MYSELF," she opines. "BUT YOUR REQUIREMENTS ARE DIFFERENT FROM OURS."

Any halfway decent explorer in my shoes, let alone a scientist, would pounce on this evidence of individual preference, and question Dizzy further about the gandy dancers' 'requirements,' whatever they may be. I do not give a feck. We have been travelling on the Ghost Train for a week, and I never thought I'd say this, but I have had enough crisp sandwiches to last me a lifetime. All I want now is to get off this horrible train. I never was a halfway decent explorer, anyway. All I ever wanted was to find something valuable enough that I could sell it and buy my own planet. If I'd ever found the Big Red Button—this is exploration industry slang for theoretical A-tech WMDs—I'd probably have put it up for auction. I'm ashamed of that, but I can admit it now.

For now I am about to *have* my own planet.

As they say, good things come to those who wait.

Yes, I wish Merrielande was a bit closer to Earth.

26,700 lightyears is a little too far to nip home for the messages.

It's in the fecking *Norma arm!*

Closer to the galactic core than to Earth!

Merrielande? Imogen's choice. It seems to mean something to her. I would have chosen something more dignified, such as New Clare.

But all that aside, it looks like a good planet.

We are in a flying saucer, de-orbiting from the local loop of the Railroad. My porthole frames Merrielande's dayside. Clouds drift over the two largest continents, which are in the southern hemisphere, separated by a strait.

"See those cloud patterns?" I say to Imogen. "That's a robust water cycle. And would you look at all those variegations in the greenery. This planet's got your full range of ecosystems, ranging from savannah to steppe, and everything in between." I catch myself thinking that surely, somewhere down there, must be a boggy coast where the waves crash in on shingle beaches, and the sun hangs around the horizon until eleven on summer evenings.

"It's also got one big drawback," Imogen says gloomily.

"Yeah?"

"It's eight kiloparsecs from Earth."

"Oh, I was forgetting about that," I say. "Well, I know the ships are getting faster all the time. But rest your mind. We should have time to get nicely settled in before anyone makes it out this far."

"Oh *ucccchh!*" She utters the sigh/snort that she resorts to when words fail her, and turns away from me, flicking through old magazines on the iPhone she got from the Wonder Wall.

We had fun with the Wonder Wall for a while. It does gadgets as well as food, clothes, kit, anything you can think of, really. Sam discovered through tireless experimentation that it will not do guns, Class A narcotics, or porn. The exception is that it will produce ammo for Caleb's 1911. That got grandfathered in because he had it on him when he was abducted.

Imogen's iPhone doesn't get a signal, of course, and yet it contains a quirky range of content dating back a hundred years. She clings to it like a security blanket.

But the charm of ordering up gadgets wore off quickly, and in the end we all agreed to take the gandy dancers up on their offer to land us on Merrielande.

"It's going to be fine," I say to Imogen. "Anyway, think of the alternative: an endless cruise around the galaxy, without drugs or porn."

"You're disgusting," she says. She doesn't get my sarcasm at all. I have to remember to speak to her as if she were an American.

"Of course I'm not interested in drugs or porn. I'm a card-carrying romantic. My only vice is you."

She shrugs.

I am sorry to report that that a couple of days ago, under the influence of a fifth of Bushmills, I tried it on with her. That did not go well. It ended with her in a flood of tears, locking herself in the cruiser and telling me through the broken passenger-side window to fuck off because I don't understand her.

I'll say.

I stare around the flying saucer, wondering if she's got her eye on one of the others. Finian is notorious for chasing everything in a skirt. It doesn't even have to be female. And he and Imogen *have* been spending a lot of time together … But he's seventy-six. It's got to be that she sees him as a father figure.

That leaves Sam. He's bouncing around in the cockpit in the middle of the flying saucer, distracting the gandy dancers. He is an immoral, uneducated master thief with a track record of killing people at the drop of a hat. At twenty-six, he's a lot younger than Imogen and myself, but maybe that's what attracts her …

I can't picture her going for a violent criminal like him. Then again, that describes me, too. *And* Imogen herself.

Jesus, I never wanted to end up like this. And I hate the way my mind's going around in jealous circles.

But it's inevitable to an extent, isn't it? There are four of us and only one is a woman. It's not a good balance.

And if we stay on Merrielande, we will be three men and one woman until the end of our days.

Imogen's right, of course: there is virtually no chance we'll ever be found by some stray explorer. It's not the sheer distance, as much as it is all the planets in between.

There are 40,000 habitable planets in the Milky Way …

All connected by the Interstellar Railroad …

Which does not come with a map.

And there's no rhyme or reason to the Railroad's layout. Within our local bubble, the Railroad hops from star to star in a more or less predictable hexacomb pattern. But further afield, it inexplicably doubles back and loops around and jumps over whole spiral arms. We've got to the Scutum-Centaurus Arm, but no one has yet managed to reach the Sagittarius Arm, which is much closer. Earth's neighborhood and a few of the spurs off Arcadia have been mapped. Beyond that, we're blundering around in the dark.

So if we stay on Merrielande, it will be a life sentence.

I look at Imogen and I look at the mountains of stuff piled in the middle of the flying saucer, all provided by the Wall, all the survival kit I've had my eye on for years, and I remind myself that this is what I've always wanted.

And then I look at Finian and Sam and I remember that for every bloody thing under the sun there is a catch.

But when we tumble out of the flying saucer onto the prairie of Merrielande's largest continent, with the sweet scent of grass in our nostrils, and a thousand little birds whirr up into the sky, everyone laughs and smiles, because it's just so bloody good to have our feet on solid ground again.

The flying saucer sits on its jackstands in the middle of a seemingly endless sea of grass. Clouds hurry across the sky like sheep scared by a car. A few hundred yards to the north, brush traces the line of a creek.

Sam goes to have a look at the creek, while I take our anti-grav sled to check out the rock formation to the east.

The gandy dancers deliberately put us down near this rock formation, saying it would provide us with shelter. It rears out of the prairie like a gigantic reddish wart. I think there are ones like this in Australia. Up close, it's grooved with vertical rifts, and the sides of the rifts are pitted with cave mouths.

I land the sled at the bottom of a rift and scramble up to the lowest cave.

Yes, this will make a grand home until we get our houses built. In fact, maybe we won't even need to build houses. I am a great believer in avoiding hard work when at all possible. The cave is dark and cool, not at all damp, and the only wildlife I encounter is some bat-analogs that fly past my head, squeaking.

I duck, panting. They reminded me for a second of the vampire butterflies on Suckass.

Not to worry. The gandy dancers say there are no dangerous animals on Merrielande, nothing bigger than a cow on this continent, anyway, and no A-tech. No alien empire ever colonized this planet. It's all ours.

I sit in the cave mouth, enjoying the silence. Being alone takes an invisible weight off my shoulders. I've always been like this, ever since I was little. I can even breathe better when I'm alone.

I light a cigarette—the Wonder Wall had no objection to providing me with a pack of Marlboros; its ban on drugs is full of holes—and pop the tab on a Pepsi. Flat as it is, the occasion seems to call for it.

I drink my Pepsi and crunch through a package of crisps, musing about gardening rotas. Then it's time to rejoin the others.

As I skim back across the prairie, I see people running around and shouting.

Ah Jesus, it never fecking ends. You could put this lot down on the beach in Waikiki and they'd find something to get in a paddy about.

But as I get closer, I see that there are *more* people running around than there should be.

In fact, there are fifteen or so of them.

And they're making concerted rushes at the flying saucer.

And grabbing our stuff.

CHAPTER 5

There are strangers grabbing our survival gear!

Rage overcomes my common sense, such as it is. I let out a vengeful shout and accelerate to the anti-grav sled's maximum speed of about 30 miles per hour. The raiders freeze when they see me coming … all except for a couple of big lads who whip out slingshots and start whirling the blessed things around their heads.

Even the slingshot warriors scatter when I charge in among them. I whip out my lightsaber and jab at them, using it like a cattleprod. It's a grand weapon, this. I call it a lightsaber because on the short setting, it looks like one of those Jedi efforts from Star Wars. The bright blue beam terrifies the raiders into a frenzy of howls.

There's no need to hurt them, as they're already running away. I wave the lightsaber around threateningly, and am rewarded by the sight of their buttocks bobbing up and down as they flee towards the river. This is not a pleasant sight. They are squat people with very large arses. I think the polite word is steatopygic. A better one would be hippo-arsed.

"YOU! Thieving! Cunts! Feck! OFF!"

I chase them a little way, jabbing my lightsaber at their big purple behinds, and then wheel back towards the flying saucer.

The raiders have left a trail of our kit all the way to the bluffs. Rising higher into the air, I see they've got boats down on the creek, curragh-type dinghies tied up under the bluffs. The most cowardly ones are scrambling into them already.

"That's right! RUN AWAY!" I shout, waving my lightsaber.

It is somewhat consoling to know that I must look like an avenging god to them, swooping around in my airborne chariot.

I zoom back to the flying saucer.

Finian stands on the steps, shading his eyes. Imogen peeks out of the hatch above him.

"Where are Dizzy and Pew Pew?" I shout. "They said this planet was uninhabited!"

The Hippo-Arses have not gone away, after all! They're reforming at the treeline on top of the bluffs.

"Are you just going to stand there while they take our stuff?"

"Sam tried to stop them," Finian says. "He got his head broken for his trouble. A good slingshot hunter is as dangerous as a man with a gun."

"And these fat-arses are good, are they?"

"Stay there and you'll find out for yourself."

I look around. The lads with the slingshots are rallying their people. One of them darts forward and shouts gobbledygook at the flying saucer. Now he's whirling his sling around his head again.

I hop off the sled and onto the stairs below Finian.

A stone bounces off the sled, exactly where I was standing, with the *crack!* of a ricocheting bullet.

I'm safe now, for the stairs are protected by the same invisible and intangible force field that stopped the flying saucer burning to a crisp in the atmosphere. It's much more advanced than the biotech force fields we discovered on the Lost Planet. Everything the gandy dancers have is better.

I moodily thumb my lightsaber off. It's got a limited range of about thirty meters. "Jesus Christ, I wish I had a gun!"

"And what would you do with it if you had?" Finian says dryly.

I'm about to reply, 'Shoot the feckers, of course,' when I feel Imogen's eyes on me. She was much more upset than I was when Sam killed those security guards on Treetop's moon. She's a vegan and all. It's the purest hypocrisy, for didn't she used to work for the Russian mob on Arcadia, and they murder people for fun and profit, but that's different, or something. Jesus, I don't know. What I do know is it's out of sight, out of mind for her, and I know something else, too. If we stay on Merrielande, the Hippo-Arses will never be out of sight, out of mind, or out of our business.

"There are too many of them to shoot," I mutter.

"You don't know the half of it," Finian says. "Apparently they evolved here, same as we evolved on Earth. They've exterminated all the megafauna on this continent and now they're migrating towards the straits, looking for new sources of game. There are about three million of them. That's according to Dizzy and Pew Pew."

F. R. SAVAGE

"I am going to murder those little twats," I say, grinding my teeth.

Speak of the devil. Dizzy and Pew Pew come down the steps behind Finian.

"You said there was nothing dangerous here!" I shout at them.

Dizzy stops, holding the railing of the steps, lightly balanced on her short legs. "WE SAID NO DANGEROUS ANIMALS. THESE NOT ANIMALS, IN INFORMAL HUMAN TAXONOMY."

"And what about 'uninhabited'?!?"

"WE SAID UNCOLONIZED. NOT UNINHABIT-ED."

While we were talking, the Hippo-Arses have returned for more plunder, the brazen gobshites. There are about thirty of them this time. The others must have been hiding in the brushwood. While the slingshot hunters keep a wary eye on the flying saucer, the rest pick up as much of our stuff as they can carry.

We brought everything on the enterprising colonist's shopping list:

- Tents
- Seeds
- Tools
- Grain grinders
- Insect-proof food storage bins
- Water purification filters
- Ovens
- A lifetime's supply of drugs and medical kit, including immune booster shots
- Radios

- Crossbows and bolts

Everything's solar-powered, of course.

- A million batteries for when the sun doesn't shine

… and the list goes on and on. I really came into my own when we were deciding what to request from the Wonder Wall. I've survived more camping trips on alien planets than the rest of this crew combined.

The Hippo-Arses, of course, have no idea what any of our stuff is. One of them sinks his chompers into the soft pillow Imogen specially requested, and spits out polyfoam filling. Another is trying to wear a string of solar panels as armor.

One of the hunters yells at them to hurry up.

I don't know what he said, but I *know* what he said, if you know what I mean.

I scowl at Dizzy and Pew Pew, with a sinking feeling in my stomach. "Are they … intelligent?"

"UNKNOWN," says Pew Pew. "WE WILL FIND OUT."

Both gandy dancers raise their right arms and hum softly.

Without warning, the smaller slingshot hunter rises into the air and floats, screeching and flailing, towards the flying saucer. He vanishes around the far side of the craft and is heard no more.

The rest have watched in gobsmacked amazement, but when the bigger slingshot hunter rises into the air in his turn, they turn tail and run.

It does them no good. One by one, the flying saucer's invisible tractor beam—the same kind of beam, I am certain, as the one that trapped our police cruiser—catches them and lifts them into the air. One by one, they vanish inside the flying saucer.

When their jabbering is silenced, peace falls once more upon the prairie.

But it's a shite kind of peace, with our kit scattered everywhere, and some of the Hippo-Arses' tree-bark waistcoats and plumed headdresses mixed in with it.

Dizzy turns to me. "DO YOU STILL WANT TO STAY HERE?"

I draw a deep breath. "You mean we still can?"

"YES, IF YOU LIKE."

I think about what that would mean. Fighting with the Hippo-Arses every bleeding day, I've no doubt. Maybe we could teach them that we're to be feared and avoided, but there are millions of them to five of us, and they have already demonstrated a fearless bent for thievery.

I dicker. "If we stay, will you give us guns, then?"

"NO."

"Why the feck not?"

"YOU HAVE CROSSBOWS."

"I only asked for those because you wouldn't give us rifles. I've never shot a crossbow in my life."

"YOU ARE SAPIENT. YOU CAN LEARN."

A laugh, quickly smothered, comes from the top of the steps. Imogen. What does she think is so funny? The gandy dancers' blatantly low opinion of our intelligence?

I grind my teeth, resisting the impulse to glance at Finian and see what he's thinking. I will make this decision myself.

"No," says Imogen, and the laughter's gone from her voice. "We're not staying. This is *their* planet, not ours."

With that, she turns and goes back into the flying saucer.

"Right," I mutter. "It looks like we're not staying."

"UNDERSTOOD, FLETCH."

Dizzy and Pew Pew hum in unison and wave their arms. As if sucked up by an invisible hoover, our kit rises into the air and arcs back into the flying saucer. Finian and I have to duck or get hit in the head by the larger pieces of equipment. Within a few moments, the prairie is pristine once more, leaving no sign we were ever here.

But on the way back up to the local loop, I remember something.

I whisper to Sam. I'm sitting next to him this time, as I'm thoroughly pissed off with Imogen. This is because, or maybe in spite of, her being right. "Guess what."

He turns a drawn face to me. The slingshot hunter's stone left a pigeon's egg on his forehead. The gandy dancers have put a white compress on it. "What?"

"I left some rubbish in that cave. A Pepsi can and an empty package of Taytos. Imagine the distant descendants of the Hippo-Arses finding that in a million years' time."

We crack up, shaking in our seats.

I leave unspoken the biggest implication of this oversight: the gandy dancers are not omniscient and omnipotent, after all.

CHAPTER 6

Back aboard the Ghost Train, Caleb greets us with obnoxious glee. It turns out he suspected the trick that Dizzy and Pew Pew played on us, but didn't say anything. "So you decided not to stay, huh? Some of 'em do stay! An' next time we visit, coupla years later, they're always daid as a goldurn doornail."

He says the gandy dancers are currently 'examining' half a dozen species, widely scattered throughout the galaxy, which have the potential to be classified as sapient.

"They brought back a bunch of those fatsos, huh? They're probably examining them right now. Wanna watch? It's freaky as all heck."

"Jesus," I say, in a very bad mood at this point, "I can't think of anything I'd less rather see than a probe being shoved up a Hippo-Arse's rear end."

But everyone else wants to see, and I trail along after them. Caleb leads the way to the lounge.

We have spent very little time here, except when getting stuff from the Wonder Wall. I thought it was queer at first that Caleb lives in his pickup truck, when the whole Ghost

Train is his oyster, but we have been doing the exact same thing. The lounge is just not welcoming somehow. So myself, Sam, and Finian have been sleeping in the Sagittarian long-distance monowheel, while Imogen reposes in relative comfort in the back of the police cruiser. Somehow, this seems preferable to sleeping in the lounge.

And now I know why. Each of the clinical white sofas has risen up to table height (for a gandy dancer), and on each of them lies a Hippo-Arse, unconscious beneath hospital lights. I shudder. Something in me suspected that this was the true purpose of the lounge all along.

There are a dozen gandy dancers here. I've never seen any of them before, not that you can tell them apart. These ones are wearing white coats like doctors. They move between the tables, poking and prodding the Hippo-Arses, murmuring in fridge-like voices.

It is now clear that Dizzy and Pew Pew, in their overalls, are mere janitors, delivery-truck drivers, or what have you. This is the crew that runs things.

Mercifully, we seem to have come too late to see the physical examinations. The Hippo-Arses snore and fart in their sleep. The gandy dancers step back, and a sarcophagus descends over each table.

Before the sarcophagi hide the Hippo-Arses from sight, I glimpse the inside of the nearest one.

It is lined with five-inch nails.

"It's an Iron Maiden!" I blurt.

"Oh no, it ain't," Caleb says. "It's a Tomb of Youth."

"A what?"

Caleb beckons us away from the entrance to the lounge, back into the stairwell. He draws us close with his skinny arms around Sam's shoulders and my own. Maybe it's the lighting, but I seem to see livid sparks dancing in his eyes, like the worms of hellfire that wriggle along the undercarriage of the Ghost Train. He says in a hoarse whisper: "How you figger I stay so young?"

Finian is the first to speak up. "You're having us on," he says, and his voice sounds old and uncertain in comparison to Caleb's sprightly hiss.

"It's the Lord's truth. I'll show you as soon as they're gone."

In another few minutes the lounge is empty of gandy dancers. Only the tables remain, lidded by sarcophagi, like sinister soup tureens.

"They'll leave 'em in the Tombs for a few hours," Caleb says. "Fix whatever's wrong with 'em. Worms, parasites, teeth problems, that's mostly what these primitives got. Then they'll let 'em out."

"You mean, they'll take them back to their planet?" Imogen says.

Caleb shows his teeth. I notice again how straight and white these are. I thought it was just American dentistry. "They'll ask 'em if they want to go back. If they do, off they go. If they want to stay here …" He mimes drawing his 1911, flipping off the safety. "I'm a get me some target practice."

Finian snorts approvingly, and Imogen smiles. I am sure neither of them believes him. They think he's taking the piss.

I meet Sam's eyes. *We* know he is not joking. If any Hippo-Arses are foolish enough to stay on the Ghost Train, Caleb will hunt them down like animals, while singing along to Johnny Cash.

He is the apex predator of this tiny ecosystem—the one human who, when abducted, happened to be carrying a gun.

"Fair play to you," I say, smiling, and thinking that I will kill him at some point. It would be safer for all of us.

The gandy dancers are out of the way but the lounge is still dim. Caleb leads us to a table with no Hippo-Arse or tureen on it. "This one musta died." He climbs onto the table and lies down, arms crossed over his chest. "That's all you gotta do."

With the faintest of hums, a sarcophagus descends from the ceiling.

Caleb rolls off the table. "I ain't goin' in just now. Don't wanna be greedy."

The Tomb of Youth stops, a few feet above the table.

"Seems like some of y'all need it more than me."

Caleb looks at Finian.

We all look at Finian—seventy-six, beer-bellied, not as quick on his feet as he used to be. He's lost none of his swagger but it has seemed to me as if he lost *something* when he exchanged the pirate lifestyle for an NEPD badge.

"It don't hurt, buddy," Caleb says gently.

For the first time I can remember, Finian seems to be lost for words.

He grunts, turns on his heel and walks away.

This is so unusual, I'm tempted to go after him. But something else has occurred to me. I lean over the table, peering up at the nail-like protrusions on the Tomb's underside.

"Careful," Caleb says.

"Sam? Do those look like what I think they are?"

He's at my side, holding the compress onto his forehead with one hand. "Oh fuuuuck."

I unzip my cargo pocket and bring out the Gizmo of Rejuvenation. I hold it up, comparing it to the nail-like protrusions on the Tomb's underside.

Imogen pushes between us. "Is that the Gizmo? Let me see."

She forgot about the Gizmo amidst the excitement of the last few days. It's understandable.

"Wow," she says, hushed. "It's the same."

"It is," I say.

Sam and I exchange an uneasy glance. When he got shot on Treetop's moon, he used the Gizmo to heal himself. It worked like a fecking charm. Bullet wounds that should have killed him vanished like marks on an erasable whiteboard. There were no side effects, except that he looked thinner afterwards. I assume the Gizmo used up his bodily reserves to repair the damage. He's back to his normal weight now, anyway, as he should be, given how much he's been eating since we got on the Ghost Train.

"So now we know where it came from," Imogen says. She stares into the Tomb of Youth, as if counting its spikes to see is there one missing. But there are about thirty Tombs. It could have come from any of them. Or it could have been part of another rejuvenation machine, made by the same aliens who built the Ghost Train, whoever they were. I think I heard that the King's explorers found it in the Scutum-Centauri arm.

Caleb goggles at the Gizmo in my hand. "Ooo-wee. You better not let the Grays know you took that." 'The Grays' is what he calls the gandy dancers, for some reason. "They would *not* be happy."

"We didn't *take* it," I say irritably.

"Yes, we did," Imogen says. "We stole it from the King, and that's how this whole disaster started."

"They got kings these days?" Caleb is occasionally curious about how the world has changed since the 20th century.

"Yes," I snap. "Dozens of them, and hundreds of barons and lords and that sort of thing. You can buy yourself a title if you've got your own planet. That's what I was going to do."

"Then maybe you should have stayed on Merrielande," Imogen says, her voice high and shaky. *"King* Fletch."

She whirls around and stomps out of the lounge.

I go after her. I don't know what I could say to cheer her up. I never get to say it, anyway, because Imogen passes Dizzy in the doorway. The little gandy dancer comes into the lounge.

I whip the Gizmo behind my back.

It's no good. Dizzy toddles towards me and holds out one three-fingered hand.

"What?" I say, looking down at her.

"GIVE ME THE ARTEFACT YOU ARE HIDING BEHIND YOUR BACK."

Sam sniggers. Then he says quietly, "Do it, Fletch. We just got a glimpse of what these guys are capable of. Pissing them off: *not* recommended."

I know he's right, but it still stings. What right have the gandy dancers got to confiscate our stuff?

Exactly as much right as they had to abduct us in the first place. Which is none at all. But they did it anyway.

I slap the Gizmo into Dizzy's hand.

"THANK YOU," she says. Then she points at the Tomb of Youth that's halfway down from the ceiling. "DO ANY OF YOU WISH TO USE THIS FACILITY?"

"No," Sam says. *"One* five-inch nail—OK, I can convince myself it's just a big needle. Hundreds of them? Sorry. Too creepy." He touches the bump on his head. "I'll let Dr. Time take care of this."

Dizzy leaves the lounge. Soon, Sam and Caleb are requesting dinner from the Wonder Wall, squabbling about the merits of curly french fries versus steak fries. It's as if we never went down to the surface of Merrielande, never abandoned hope of getting off the Ghost Train.

Back on the road again.

CHAPTER 7

Sam and Caleb get dinner from the Wonder Wall, and Imogen comes back from the parking lot, a bit tearstained, to join them. Strangely, I'm not hungry at the moment.

I leave them to it and catch up with Finian on the observation deck.

He's sat on one of the benches facing the front of the train, staring out. "Here you go." I set down a couple of glasses and pour from my new bottle of Bushmills.

"That's the core of the galaxy," he says, nodding at the windows.

The glow ahead of us looks like a crack in the darkness of the universe. It's so bright we don't need any other light to see by. It's been like this for the last couple of days. That keen astronomer Caleb tells us it is the Galactic Bar. And we are rushing towards it.

"Boldly going where, blah blah blah," I sigh. I plonk down beside Finian and sip my whisky. "Maybe we should have stayed on Merrielande, after all."

I'm inviting him to blame our hasty decision on me. I want him to show some bloody leadership. Yes, I know I've complained about his tyrannical ways in the past, but it turns out that worse than a tyrant is a tyrant who's stepped down from his pedestal.

"Do you know why I joined the NEPD?" He opens one huge, age-spotted fist. There's his NEPD sherriff's star, laminated with unbreakable A-tech glass.

"Was it something that happened on the Omega Centauri spur? I heard it was a bit of a shambles."

"Heh. It was a fecking omnishambles. There were the lads and myself in three of Special Delivery Sam's own ships, her expecting them back, not expecting us at all. We gave her a beating to start with. You can't really go wrong with a surprise attack on a planet. But she had thousands of people out there. They retreated into the hills, and it turned into a ground war, and they knew the ground better than we did. Omega Centauri 49 is like Wales with more mountains, if you can picture such a thing. It rains all the bleeding time. My lads were getting picked off, and we were living on potatoes … sure it's a thrilling life being a pirate. And I dropped my lightsaber into a river. If I was superstitious, I'd say I lost my luck at that point."

My uncle is one of the most superstitious people I know.

"How did it end up, then?" I already know, actually. I just haven't heard it from him.

"Oh, those bastards from Samsung called in the army on us. Woke up one morning and the sky was full of fecking Sukhois."

That was the first time the military ever left our solar system. "You know you've made it when they alter government policy for you," I offer.

"Oh, it wasn't me they were after, it was the force fields."

"I thought it was Special Delivery Sam."

"No, she was collateral damage as well. They were there to enforce Samsung's claim to the force fields discovery."

"So you and her got caught in the same net." As I thought, they must have given Finian a choice between going straight and going to prison. "That was right before they set up the NEPD …"

"Yeah. They decided they needed an option in between doing nothing and sending in the military."

"And is that why you joined?"

He gives me a death's-head grin. "No, lad. It was for the health benefits."

I'm halfway into a laugh when I realize he means it.

"I've got lung cancer."

"Ah, shite."

He nods. "They've given me six months."

"Can they not do anything for it? What about those drugs that attack cancer cells?"

"They don't work if you've let it metastasize on account of not seeing a proper doctor in years."

"You don't even smoke."

"I used to."

It's true, he was a fearsome chimney when I was working for him on the Draco spur.

"Are you taking the drugs, though?"

"I am, sure. I *was,* anyway."

Before we got abducted by the Ghost Train.

"Have you asked the Wonder Wall to whip you up some generics? It did the drugs we wanted to take to Merrielande. I've got … erm … cigarettes out of it and all."

Something flashes across Finian's face. Probably the reference to cigarettes. But all he says is, "Fletch, the drugs aren't going to cure me. I'm too far gone. The only thing that works is the painkillers."

He shows me a couple of pills, and downs them with a mouthful of whisky.

"Just what the doctor ordered," he says with a haggard smile.

I put down my glass. "Finian, you've got to go in one of those things."

"Those tombs?"

"Yeah, whatever they are. The technology obviously works. Caleb's a hundred and thirty-five years old, he looks sixty. *He* ought to be dead from cancer by now, the amount of fried food he eats."

Finian shakes his head, and I know what I'm up against: the solid granite wall of his superstition.

I argue with him, half-heartedly, and after a few minutes I get up on the excuse that I've got to go for a slash. I leave him hunched over his whisky glass, staring into the core of the galaxy.

Back in the parking lot, the others are cooped up inside the Sagittarian monowheel, watching a film on the telly we got from the Wonder Wall. Quietly, I retrieve Finian's metalforma knife from the place where I hid it days ago under the wrecked Denebite space shuttle. He never even asked me what happened to it. That shows how demoralized he is.

But he will not refuse a go with the Gizmo of Rejuvenation.

It's not like I'll be asking him to lie down inside a sarcophagus lined with nails. That would put anyone off. It certainly did me.

It's just a little injection.

That's how Sam did it.

He stuck the Gizmo into his side, and boom, it healed him of gunshot wounds that should have killed him.

If it could do that, it can certainly knock out a few measly cancer cells.

With the metalforma knife in my waistband, I hurry back up the stairs to the lounge.

Dizzy took our Gizmo, but I can get another one just the same. There are thousands of them.

The lights are still dim, the Hippo-Arses still encased in their Tombs of Youth, and the Tomb that Caleb summoned is still hanging above a table with no one on it.

I'm six foot one in my sock feet. I can just about reach the inner edge of the Tomb if I balance one knee on the edge of the table.

Bracing my left hand on the outside of the Tomb, I apply the metalforma knife's blade to one of the spikes. I could use my lightsaber, of course, but I'm not sure what these spikes are made of. Energy sometimes interacts with energy in unpredictable ways. The knife's a safer bet.

Metalforma is an A-tech material, originally found on a planet called Basilisk, which must have been inhabited by serial killers with warped minds. It changes shape when pressure is applied, sending out thousands of wee spikes and tendrils. These fracture the target material at the atomic level, as well as slicing through it on the macro level. I've seen a metalforma knife used to cut through solid artificial diamond.

Whatever these spikes are made of, they aren't *that* tough.

Flakes fall on the table, followed by a whole five-inch spike, which now has a jagged thick end.

I snatch it up with my sleeve over my hand. Into my pocket it goes. Finian never examined our Gizmo very closely. He won't know the difference.

So I'll tell him this is the Gizmo we stole from King Zuckerberg, and what's good enough for Zuck's filthy-rich friends should be good enough for him. Anyway, it's only a wee injection …

This is as far as I get in my thinking before I'm lifted off my feet.

The lights go on.

The white-coated gandy dancers troop into the lounge. Dizzy, in the lead, is holding her arm up in that Heil Hitler gesture.

I'm borne over their heads, bellowing and kicking helplessly. Then a mighty shock jolts my body and everything goes black.

CHAPTER 8

I've woken up in some awful places in my time. On a planet covered with giant geraniums (Suckass, of evil memory); face-down and hungover in a desert where every bloody thing evolved from spiders (that was when I was working for Finian); and in a field behind the house of the girl I was seeing in fifth year, with her auld fella standing over me, on his way to let out the cows. I was so drunk that after she sent me on my way, I slipped on a cowpat and passed out where I fell.

But all those awakenings compare favorably to this one.

My back is breaking. I'm hanging spreadeagled with four squashy cuffs around my ankles and wrists. Each cuff is attached to a rod perpendicular to my body, so I can't move.

I'm looking down into a psychedelic soup bowl of swirling colors where shapes appear and vanish. It's like one of those pin art toys everyone had when we were little. You and your friends would press your faces into it and laugh at the impressions you made. Except these impressions are the colors of curry vomit and they are the shape of pyramids, poking up and collapsing.

When I blink, the concave bowl turns into a convex sphere.

Blurred stars twinkle above its limb.

It's a fecking *planet*.

I'm hanging above an unknown planet, at less than Railroad height. *Much* less. This is satellite height, barely out of the atmosphere.

And actually, I've not got a spacesuit on, so I should be dead.

Oh, right. Advanced force fields.

Jesus, my back!

I flex my limbs, trying to take the weight off my tortured spine, and above me I hear a bitter laugh.

"How does it feel to be too stupid to live?"

Imogen!

With a huge effort, I twist my head to see over my shoulder.

Above me floats the pearly belly of a flying saucer, maybe the same one we rode down to Merrielande. I'm suspended at an angle to the hatch. Imogen sits on the lip of the hatch with her arms wrapped around her knees.

"Help me," I gasp.

She shakes her head slowly. There's anger on her face, but also resolve. It's the latter which makes my teeth chatter with fear.

"We *barely* made it into the sapient category, you know," she says. "Dizzy and Pew Pew showed me our test scores. We don't stack up to the Klingons, or the Sagittarians, or even the Denebites."

"Help me. Please, Imogen. My back's breaking."

"As for the Silicon People? Forget it. They were the

smartest aliens who ever lived. Their brains were super-computers. Actually, this was their home planet." Her voice shakes. "Isn't it pretty?"

I might call it *pretty* if I were much, much further away. Up close, it is a nightmare vision. I can't even put names to the colors of those clouds.

And now the clouds are bulging. A blue-gray thunderhead climbs towards us like a punching fist. It rears hundreds of miles high, and then crashes back into piss-yellow froth.

"Oh fuck," Imogen says, shivering. "It almost got us that time."

Dizzy appears beside Imogen. "THOSE NOT CLOUDS," she says. "THIS NOT PLANET. ONE POINT FOUR BILLION EARTH YEARS AGO, PLANET FORMERLY OCCUPYING THIS VOLUME WAS CONSUMED BY QUASI-SENTIENT SWARM OF NANOMACHINES. GGXKT'VA, CALLED SILICON PEOPLE IN ENG-LISH, WERE CONSUMED, TOO."

"They weren't that smart, so," I grit.

"HAVE YOU HEARD OF SINGULARITY? GGXKT'VA ENGINEERED OWN SINGULARITY. PLAN WAS UPLOADING SELF-BRAINS INTO NANOSWARM." I hear an unfamiliar crackling noise. It is Dizzy laughing. "SMARTEST BEINGS MAKE BIGGEST MISTAKES. THIS IS PARADOX OF INTELLIGENCE."

Imogen leans down towards me, her dark shoulder-length hair hanging on either side of her face. "They're *still in there!*" she hisses. "They uploaded themselves … into *hell.*"

She draws back.

"Do you want to get off here, Fletch?" Her voice shakes. "Really, I mean, it's *your choice.* Would you like to get off?"

53

She's angry with me. She's fuming. It's about Merrielande. It's about our dashed hopes. It's about the mess I've dragged her into, when all she wanted was a normal life. "Jesus, Imogen!" I twist helplessly in my bonds. "I'm sorry Merrielande went to shite! I apologize, it's all my fault, but you can't blame me for the Hippo-Arses! If the bleeding gandy dancers had told us they were there—"

"If the gandy dancers had given you weapons like you wanted, you'd have murdered them all!"

Yes actually, I would, and I'd not have lost any sleep over it. Well. Not much.

"You think just because they're barely-intelligent aliens, they don't deserve to live! But maybe *we're* the barely-intelligent aliens who don't deserve to live. " Suddenly, tears spill from her eyes. She leans across the hatch. That's my metalforma knife in her hand. I can't see what she's doing, but I find out when the rods attached to my wrists give way, one after the other. Metalforma can cut through anything.

I plunge head-down. Now I'm hanging by my ankles. My arms flail.

"How does it feel to be *helpless,* Fletch?"

Everything falls out of my pockets. The Gizmo of Rejuvenation—that is, the one I hacked off the sarcophagus, bringing down this terrible punishment on myself. My lightsaber! I've had that for more than twenty years. There it goes, tumbling end over end, down towards the planet-sized nanoswarm.

Finian said that when he lost his lightsaber he lost his luck. I get the feeling I lost my luck a long time ago. On the day I met Imogen, perhaps.

"The way you feel right now," she shouts, "is the way I've felt all my life."

I crane my neck and see her leaning out of the hatch.

"It fucking sucks, doesn't it, Fletch?"

"Yes, Imogen. It fucking sucks." I try to mirror her diction exactly, without a hint of sarcasm. "Please don't kill me."

Unless they've ordered her to. Unless this is *her* punishment. For what? For associating with me.

Tears glitter on her face. She leans out further. Now it's her iPhone in her hand. "I'm just going to take a few pictures." Her voice shakes. "If I ever get a signal again, I'll submit them to the Darwin Awards."

Click, click, and the stupid clumsy bitch drops her phone.

She rears back, crying, "Dizzy! Dizzy, my phone!"

The iPhone hits me on the hip and falls past me.

Down below, the planet-sized nanoswarm extrudes a green-and-black cyclone. It lashes upwards like a whip, reaching for the phone.

Dizzy pushes Imogen aside. She raises her arm and hums. The iPhone reverses course and rises up towards the flying saucer, past me. It floats back to Imogen, who clasps it gratefully. "I'm so sorry, Dizzy."

"BE MORE CAREFUL."

"I will."

"WHAT DO YOU WISH TO DO ABOUT FLETCHER? IT IS YOUR CHOICE. THE DECISION YOU MAKE NOW WILL HELP US DETERMINE WHETHER YOUR SPECIES IS WORTHY TO INHERIT THE GALAXY."

And even with the blood rushing to my head, even hanging upside-down above a planet-sized swarm of silicon ghosts that'd eat the flesh off my bones before I ever reached the ground, if there is any ground down there at all, I find a moment to be outraged. Who the hell appointed these soulless little robots to sit in judgement over us?

Imogen neatly dodges the question. She says, "No, it's *his* choice." She leans down again—holding onto her phone very tightly this time. "What did you say, Fletch? Do you want to get off? I didn't hear you. What did you say?"

"I don't want to get off," I say, looking up into her eyes. "Imogen, I don't want to get off here."

She smiles, wetly. "Good."

Dizzy stretches down a strong three-fingered hand and pulls me up through the hatch, to safety.

On the way back to the train, Imogen and I sit close together, not quite cuddling, but something like that. Both of us are limp with exhaustion. I don't know exactly what just happened, but I know I'm alive. That's what counts. I also know I should be angry with Imogen, but I can't muster any rage at the small, soft, tearstained bundle resting against my side. I am also aware of how much I don't understand at the moment. Any rant that I went off on, I might be barking up the wrong tree, further confusing the situation, when we've only just made it up.

Yes, I know. *Too stupid to live* sums it up nicely.

Her head rests against the top of my arm. She clings to her iPhone, as usual. I suppose it represents the whole of human civilization to her now.

Are we worthy to inherit the galaxy? Obviously not. But that's not the point. Why do the gandy dancers get to decide?

"Can I see those pictures?" I say. "Must be gas."

Imogen instinctively clutches the iPhone away from me.

"I won't delete them. Promise."

This time, she gets my sarcasm. She gives me a tiny, secretive grin. Flick flick go her eyes, making sure Dizzy and Pew Pew are busy in the cockpit.

Shielding the screen with her hand, she opens the iPhone's pictures folder and shows me …

Nothing. The folder's empty.

"I wasn't taking pictures of you," she breathes into my ear. "I was taking pictures of that planet. Ex-planet. Whatever."

"What for?"

"Well, not exactly taking pictures. When I ordered this phone, I asked for wide-bandwidth wireless data transfer functionality."

"Huh?"

She shrugs. Her expression says I'm being stupid again. I suppose I am. My shoulder joints ache like hell, and I've got a fearsome headache.

Back on board the Ghost Train, the sorting of the Hippo-Arses has been completed. Some of them are on their way back to their home planet, I assume. Others must have seen the Wonder Wall, and decided to stick around. Look at all this lovely A-tech, Ugg. Yeah, let's take advantage, Grok. The galaxy clearly has a lot to offer Hippo-Arses of superior smarts and daring.

The paradox of intelligence. I think that was the phrase Dizzy used.

The parking bay echoes with gunshots, whoops, and cries of terror from Hippo-Arses who thought they were smart.

One of them lies in the aisle near the police cruiser. He,

or she, is bleeding out from a gunshot wound. Imogen's fingers dig into my wrist. We circle as widely around the dying Hippo-Arse as the narrow aisle allows.

"Why do the gandy dancers allow Caleb to shoot them?" I say.

"Survival of the smartest," Imogen says. "That's why they made me punish you, instead of doing it themselves. It's their hands-off approach." Her pretty lips draw back in what looks uncommonly like a snarl.

We sit in the back of the police cruiser. In the intervals between bursts of gunfire, Waylon Jennings sings *Mamas, Don't Let Your Babies Grow Up to be Cowboys*. Finian and Sam must have joined Caleb's hunt. This strikes me as another example of the kind of stupidity that might doom our species. I might actually have gone out there and tried to stop them, but I'm too tired and sort. Anyway, I can't go anywhere with Imogen snuggled up beside me, one hand on my thigh, making sure I don't desert her.

"It was an intelligence test," she says.

"What? Us versus the Hippo-Arses?"

"No, idiot. Me versus you." Suddenly she's shaking my thigh. "So I had to act stupid, don't you see? I had to pretend I was mad enough to kill you. What do you think? Was I convincing?"

She starts to cry, real tears now, not the crocodile tears she shed on the flying saucer when I was dangling 250 miles above hell.

I hold her, stroking her hair. I've said it before but it bears repeating: I don't understand her at all.

BLAM! BLAM! BLAM! Caleb must have ordered up a year's supply of ammo in advance.

Eventually the gunfire dies down. Sam dances back to the cruiser, bearing a grisly trophy: an antenna snapped off some alien spacecraft, with the head of a Hippo-Arse impaled on it. "I think this is the motherfucker who dinged me," he crows. "I just wanted to show you before I throw it out."

"It's lovely, Sam," I say, as if to a son.

He doesn't know what happened to me while they were hunting. I decide he's better off not knowing, and not merely because I don't want to talk about it. Imogen's hints have set off my dodgy-business radar. When I work out what she's been hinting around, and whether it is harmful to the rest of us, I will tell Sam. Not before.

We go with him to the other end of the parking bay. This is where the rubbish hatches and the toilets are located. We tend to stay clear of this area, as it smells.

The gandy dancers drag Hippo-Arse corpses to the hatches. In they go, one after the other.

Caleb watches with addled pride. "Fourteen," he gloats. "I got four*teen* of those mofos!"

"Did you get any?" I say to Finian, who's standing by, hands in his pockets.

He shakes his head. "Wasn't in the mood," and my worries about his health return.

"NOW WATCH THIS," says Pew Pew. He adjusts his fedora.

The whole wall around the rubbish hatches goes transparent. For an instant I see a fecking *mountain* of rubbish, including all the gear we had the Wonder Wall make for our trip to Merrielande.

Then it's gone, tumbling down towards the malevolent

orb of the Silicon People's home planet.

"WE USE AS RUBBISH DUMP," Pew Pew says. "EVEN CATASTROPHIC MISTAKES OF HIGHLY INTELLIGENT SPECIES HAVE SILVER LINING."

Finian laughs. "Sometimes I suspect you lads of having a sense of humor."

I suspect them of being robots with very warped programming. But I smile along with him. I used to fear and resent Finian. But now that I know how ill he is, that's changed. Now I need to protect him from whatever lies ahead for all of us.

CHAPTER 9

"Behold the galactic core," says Caleb with the air of a proud explorer showing off his latest find.

I thought I'd had my fill of spectacular views, but now I cringe in awe. The stars are so close together that they merge into a single ellipse of light, fringed by a milky aurora of gases. It's so bright that it blacks out the rest of the sky. The outer arms of the galaxy, including our own Orion arm and faraway Earth, might as well have been wiped out of existence. The Railroad stretches ahead of us, a gleaming bridge into the heart of the light.

It would take a poet to do justice to this, a Yeats or a Heaney. Finian's got to see it. I jog back along the moving walkway to look for him, barricading dark fears out of my mind.

He's in the lounge, button-pushing at the Wonder Wall. As I enter, I hear him saying: "Experidine ... three hundred milligrams of nooracetam ... and what was it, two hundred of desipramine. Ah, make it four hundred." The hatch opens. Finian reaches in and takes out a paper cup. "Ah Fletch," he says without missing a beat. "I was just getting my pills."

The paper cup's full of different-colored tablets and capsules. He's been trying everything the last few days. I think it's a relief for him to have the cat out of the bag, so he doesn't have to pretend anymore. Imogen's been mother-henning him, forcing him to drink all sorts of weird herb teas, which is kill or cure, as Finian told her, and he makes her try all the teas first to make sure they're not poisonous.

He now instructs me to order one of her tea recipes from the Wonder Wall. I juggle two steaming cups as we walk back to the observation deck. I've got my Bushmills sticking out of my cargo pocket. That's all that's in there now.

"So we're almost there, are we?" Finian says.

"Yeah, that's what Caleb says. He's looking forward to it."

"A layover," Finian says with contempt. This is what the gandy dancers have promised us.

Caleb welcomes us onto the observation deck, holding his guitar by the neck. "Just in time!"

My jaw drops. In the few minutes I was away, we've zoomed hundreds of lightyears closer to the galactic core. The Ghost Train is picking up speed the closer we get. Dizzy and Pew Pew explained why, although the reason escapes me now. Anyway, we're deep in the central parsec. Old red giants and new massive stars blaze on all sides.

Dead ahead, a disk of intensely bright blue gas spirals around the center of the galaxy, with twin jets of flame shooting out on the perpendicular.

"Star pulp," says Imogen in a whisper. "That's what that is. Plasma juiced out of crushed stars."

Even I, no scientist, know what's in the middle of that gas disk.

The heart of the Milky Way is a heart of darkness.

Sagittarius A*.

A supermassive black hole with the mass of four million suns.

You know these things, but it's so very different seeing them with your own eyes.

Without taking my eyes off the view, I set down the cups of tea and unscrew the cap of my Bushmills. I drink straight from the bottle.

A short distance ahead, the Railroad joins the stupendous gas accretion disk. That's where we're going. Jesus have mercy.

"INCORRECT," says Dizzy.

"What?" Imogen shouts at her, as shaken as the rest of us. "What is fucking incorrect, you condescending little robot?"

"NOT DEAD STAR PULP. JUST STRAY GAS MOL-ECULES. SAG A* IS NOT FEEDING. SOME GALAX-IES HAVE ACTIVE NUCLEI. THESE ARE CALLED FEEDING BLACK HOLES. SAG A* IS INACTIVE TYPE."

I can feel Imogen's frustration. I am not in the mood for a physics lesson, either.

But apparently we're all going to get one. Up close and personal

Blue light fills the observation desk, blinding us until the windows recalibrate their filters to spare our eyes. The Ghost Train zooms into the gas accretion disk around Sag-ittarius A*, and slaloms inwards like a rubber ducky circling the drain. Whether we like it or not, we're all about to learn how it feels to get sucked into a supermassive black hole.

I cling to the thought that the Ghost Train *does* come back, every two years like clockwork. So it must have done this countless times before, and survived, and Caleb's survived with it. But he's now looking very leery, his eyes rolling like a wild dog's.

"I've got your borrin here," he yaps at Finian.

"It's a *bodhran*," Finian says inattentively.

"And here's your whistles." Caleb thrusts a pair of tin whistles at Sam and Imogen.

Incredible as it is to recollect now, we've been whiling away the time with sessions. Neither Sam nor Imogen have an instrument, but anyone can play a tin whistle, so I got a couple out of the Wonder Wall for them, and Finian ordered himself a bodhran. When I first heard him lay the stick to the skin, the years fell away and I remembered sitting on my dad's knee in O'Donoghue's, sucking sherbet sugar off my fingers, enraptured by the music and the clapping. It was hot and dark and smoky and there was Finian in the corner where they'd shoved the tables back, joining in on the bodhran with some locals who fancied themselves the next Planxty. His hair and beard were yellow then. Even my dad clapped. He said to my mum, "And tomorrow he'll be away off to outer space again. Jesus, what a waste." I didn't understand what he meant then. I do now.

I do *not* understand why Caleb wants us to strike up a tune while we plunge into a supermassive black hole. But he's dead serious. He strums chords on his guitar. "Come on! Come on! Let's do that gospel song we been practisin'!"

Completely loony.

"Why?" says Sam, humoring the madman.

"It helps with the stretchin'!"

An instant later I get it. My body's being stretched vertically. My head feels too far away from my feet. I've not had *that* much to drink today …

"OK," Sam says. "Gotcha. It's like counting backwards from a hundred while you get whipped." He had a terrible childhood. "OK, OK …" His face furrowed with pain, he puts his tin whistle to his lips.

They're all on the floor now. Or so it looks to me. Everything's so far away.

"My life flows on!" Caleb screeches. "In endless song! Above Earth's lamentation …"

That's not a gospel song. It's a hymn I remembered from Lisdoonvarna, one of the few tunes all of us know.

"I hear the real! But far-off hymn!"

The light's overwhelming the filters, flooding the observation deck. I have to do something.

"That hails a new creation!"

Well, why not? I give the nod to Finian. He starts up the beat, and I roll out the verses.

> *Above all the tumult and the strife*
> *I hear the music ringing;*
> *It finds an echo in my soul—*
> *How can I keep from singing?*

I can see the light even with my eyes closed. My body is a million miles long. I'm a jellyfish spread across the stars.

But it's an illusion, an illusion, an illusion. I still have air in my lungs, and I stubbornly keep turning the air into words.

> *No storm can shake my inmost calm*
> *While to that rock I'm clinging;*
> *Since Christ is Lord of heaven and earth,*
> *How can I keep from singing?*

Just when I think I'm about to disintegrate into interstellar dust, the stretching goes into reverse. I'm shrinking back to my proper size. Hallelujah! From now on I'll be a different man. No more lying, cheating, stealing, or miscellaneous dodgy behavior. They won't know me in Lisdoonvarna.

(I have these fits of insanity from time to time. I always get over them.)

The sound of Caleb's guitar dies away. I open my eyes on the ordinary dimness of the observation deck. Finian sits at my feet, slumped over his bodhran, still rattling out a drunken beat.

Dizzy and Pew Pew laugh at us. "THAT IS WORST PERFORMANCE WE EVER HEAR."

Caleb sits up and says with dignity, "That's 'cos you ain't heard me and Fletch doin' *Amazing Grace* with half a bottle a whiskey each inside us."

Sam is on his knees, throwing up.

I heave Finian to his feet and get him to sit down on the nearest bench. "Where're your pills …?"

Imogen stands at the table with a cupped hand raised to her mouth. She swallows, sees me watching her, and looks away hurriedly.

She's taken Finian's pills.

All that's left is one cup of herb tea.

Too bemused to question her behavior, I give the remaining cup of tea to Finian.

"Where's the milk and sugar?" he says, as he always does. He's all right.

"I have a question," I say to the gandy dancers. "What's that?"

That is the star now visible ahead of us in the darkness. The Railroad shoots straight towards it. I would take it for an ordinary main-spectrum star, like our sun, if I didn't know that we are now inside the event horizon of a black hole. That being the case, it seems wise to question everything.

"THAT IS A STAR."

"Really." I thought we were saiing through the ordinary darkness of space, but now I notice something queer. There are *no* other stars in sight. Only this one … and the black dot of a single planet traversing across its face.

"WE ARE IN A POCKET UNIVERSE," Pew Pew says.

"OK," Imogen says, with a rather wild laugh. "I know the theory. So pocket universes really exist. Wow."

"POCKET UNIVERSE, SINGULAR. THIS IS THE ONLY ONE."

"OK. Still; wow."

Caleb, back to his bumptious self, says, "Don't worry! Getting in's a lot harder than getting out. I been here thousands of times."

I am not reassured. "So where's this famous train station?"

We are zooming closer to the lonely star all the time. Now we hurtle towards the single planet orbiting it. The sunlit curve of its surface is dusty brown. It looks like an old planet, a dead planet, like Arcadia, a planet where every trace of life was long ago bombed into dust.

"THERE," says Pew Pew, confirming my worst fears.

The Railroad curves in around the planet, and we hurtle in with it. But this is no ordinary local loop. We're diving closer to the surface all the time. We whip across the nightside, where no lights are to be seen.

"I want to go home," Sam says—the first words he's uttered since we got inside Sagittarius A*. Shut up, Sam, I think, you're not being helpful.

The Railroad shoots back into the sunlight. Sandstone-colored scabs bulge from the rocky surface of the planet. We're so low now that it's like looking down—from the cockpit—from an airplane coming in to land. The scabs are walled cities. The buildings within the walls connect to each other by flying bridges, and the highest ones sprout twin horns, a pattern which rings a bell. I've seen decorative horns like that before.

The Railroad crosses a flat silver sea. On the far shore, it swoops down to kiss the ground. We come to rest outside the walls of a city, near a towering gateway with no gate in it.

"WELCOME," says Pew Pew, "TO PRON, HOME PLANET OF THE SAGITTARIANS."

CHAPTER 10

Well, after all that, it would be daft to just stay on the train.

Imogen, however, does just that. She hides in our police cruiser, and no amount of cajoling and teasing will persuade her to come out.

Giving up, I join Finian, Sam, and Caleb on the platform. This is a ledge of reddish rock which runs along the foot of the city wall. It was the easiest disembarkation ever. We just walked out through the now-transparent wall of of the parking bay.

The air is chilly, and so dry it tickles my throat. Here and there stand signs which flicker through a dozen languages before settling on "THIS WAY." Arrows point towards the gateway.

As we walk along the length of the Ghost Train, gandy dancers swarm out and clamber all over its hull. I should think it does need maintenance. It's after plunging through a black hole, isn't it? The gandy dancers pay no attention to us. Dizzy and Pew Pew haven't come with us, either, which I must say is a relief.

"I wonder if there's a McDonald's here?" Sam jokes. He's

bounced back quickly from puking and wanting to go home. It's wonderful being in your twenties, I remember.

"I wonder how far we are from the nearest pub," Finian says.

"Hee, hee!" Caleb cackles. "You guys are gonna love this place!"

We reach the nose of the Ghost Train, which is pointing up the far side of a dip in the Railroad like the bottom of a flattened U. Beyond the tracks, a barren slope descends to the sea. I saw a film about the Dead Sea once. It's so salty nothing can live in there. The sea of Pron looks like that.

On our side of the tracks, the city's three-storey-high gateway frames a long, empty street flanked by towering buildings. It's a city built for giants. This is not surprising, as the Sagittarians *were* giants. An average adult stood twenty-two feet tall. We know this from skeletons found here and there, usually on battlefields. They were vicious customers, almost as bad as the Silicon People, judging by the number of planets they ruined. Thank God they're all dead now.

I walk under the arch of the gateway. My footsteps echo, and yet the echoes are flat and muffled. It's the dead feeling of this planet. Dead weather, dead air. Sure it's only a matter of time until we find the dead aliens.

"It's grand being masters of the galaxy," I say cynically. I have had this same sensation before, on other dead planets, and there've been too many of them. Finian's pinched expression mirrors my thoughts. We inherited the Milky Way, and now we've penetrated to the very core of the galaxy, to a pocket universe that no one knew existed … and it's the same old, fecking same old.

Everything's dead.

"Hello, travellers! How can I help you today?"

We spin around as one—all except Caleb, who cackles. *He* knew this was coming.

An invisible door has opened in the wall of the building nearest the gate. It's a normal-sized door, a *human*-sized door, and in it stands a creature that's roughly human-sized ... but definitely not human.

It has green scaly skin, a small horn on the top of its bald head, and a ridiculously over-developed upper body. With its barrel chest and short legs, it looks like a cartoon body-builder. Its red, slit-pupiled eyes gleam with incalculable malice. It is wearing navy tracksuit bottoms and a white polo shirt, and carrying a tablet computer, one clawed finger poised over the screen.

"Jesus," says Finian, "it's a Draconian."

The remains of these aliens are often found in the same places as Sagittarian remains. It's thought they were the Sagittarians' arch-enemies.

"Did you win, then?" Finian says.

"No," snaps the Draconian. "We lost. And I asked you a question. Can I help you today?"

It manages to make every one of the last three words sound like a four-letter one.

"Ah, well, sure, in that case, can I have a Guinness?" Finian says. "If you've got it on draft, mind. None of that canned shite."

"Only Budweiser. In cans."

"That'll do us," I say, before Finian can piss the Draconian off any further.

"I'll have a Coke," Sam chimes in.

Caleb has been enjoying our confusion. Wiping away

tears of laughter, he manages, "Let's go into the bar."

With many backward glances on my part, we follow the Draconian into the cathedral-sized building. Huge carved pillars support the roof of a dark dusty hall. Another human- or reptilian-sized door on the far side leads into a fug of warmth and light. There's the noise of talk, and a deafening clamor like a toddler banging on saucepans with a spoon, which I realize is probably the alien equivalent of muzak.

Have you ever seen the original Star Wars, from the 20th century? Remember the scene in the bar?

This is nothing like that.

At all.

Yes, it is a bar, I suppose. And yes, it is full of aliens of every species known to humanity, and some not.

But no one stops talking when we come in. A couple of them glance around with scant interest and then go back to watching television.

There is a Sagittarian-sized television-analog device at the end of the bar. That's where the saucepan-and-spoons noise is coming from.

"They're a bit hard of hearing," Caleb shouts over the racket.

"Why is that?" Sam shouts back.

"Well, they're all pretty old." And Caleb sits back and shakes with glee.

The Draconian plonks down out drinks, including a rum and Coke for Caleb. He didn't even have to order. They know him here.

I turn and survey the alien company once more. Yes, there are Puzzlers. There are Klingons. There are Denebites, with four arms and fierce beaked visages. I dressed up as a Denebite for King Zuck's fancy dress party. I cringe at the memory. There are Krells, and there is a single solitary Silicon Person, floating by itself on a gravsled.

All the other aliens are also floating on mobility devices. Convergent evolution applies to machines, too. Their floating couches and chairs look very much like the anti-grav mobility chairs that have made handicapped, elderly, and morbidly obese people the terrors of Earth's skies.

The Denebites are using walkers. Makes sense when you have four arms.

The truth sinks in. "It's a flipping nursing home," I say. "The Nursing Home at the Core of the Galaxy. Comfortable rooms, exercise facilities, bathing nearby, a community lounge, and round-the-clock care by a highly trained staff of Draconians. This is where aliens come to die after they've rampaged themselves out of business. Am I missing anything?"

"Yeah," Caleb says. He points at the end of the room where the television is not. "Him."

I squint into the shadows, and as I make out what's back there, my blood runs cold.

Sitting on an enormous throne, knees wide apart, gripping the horned armrests, and glaring in *our direction,* is a Sagittarian.

He sees me looking at him. His lips, thin and black in a goatish face, draw back in a terrifying leer. He leans forward—it's like one of those horrible gigantic Soviet statues of Stalin or somebody leaning down from its pedestal—and the black birds sitting on his horns flutter up in a rustle of ragged wings. The talk around the television goes quiet *then.*

It's uncanny how much the Sagittarians looked like medieval pictures of Lucifer.

Look, Fletch, my boy. *Look* at him.

He's not dead at all.

Jesus, I wish this planet *had* turned out to be just another graveyard littered with skeletons.

I sip Budweiser from the can. I've seldom been so shook. I can feel the Sagittarian's malevolent gaze on the back of my neck, prickling.

Our Draconian waiter comes back and drops into a chair at our table without being asked. "They won the war," it says morosely. "We lost. And that's how we ended up here, slaving for *him.* Before you ask, there are worse fates, and I'm fanatically loyal to my master, as a Draconian should be. So don't even think about asking me where he keeps the good stuff."

"Where does he keep the good stuff?" Sam asks immediately.

An older hand than Sam, I am not going to fall for that one. "What worse fates?"

"Sss?" says the Draconian, obviously meaning, "Huh?"

"What's a worse fate than slaving for a Sagittarian pub owner?"

"Planet owner. *Planet* owner."

"Sorry."

There aren't supposed to be any living aliens. Humanity is currently the only sapient species in the universe. All the scientists agree on that. It's what I was taught in school and all.

Cognitive dissonance smashes into me like a wave of the sea, and recedes. I can't argue with the evidence of my eyes.

And my nose. I can smell the Sagittarian from here, a faint but distinct carrion reek.

I say to the Draconian, "I'm just trying to imagine what could be a worse fate than this." And I am thinking that the gandy dancers said we would be here for twenty-seven hours, and I will make sure we get back on board in plenty of time, because if we get left behind on Pron, I think I would have to kill myself. Even though the Budweiser, or clever-clogs advanced-science simulation thereof, is no more disgusting than American beer usually is.

."What could be worse? What could be worse? *That!*" The Draconian nods at the other aliens grouped around the television. "The Ordeal of Excruciating Tedium! They're watching recordings of victorious Sagittarian battles. That's *all there is to watch*. Over and over, every day, for billions of years."

The timescales involved boggle the mind. It's lucky we are beings of mediocre intelligence or we might be going mad at this point.

"It's the worst torture known to man, reptilian, or other sentient species," says the Draconian. "At least *we* have work to do. On which note, I have dishes to wash." It stands up.

"Wait," Finian says. "Why do you get special treatment? Weren't you the Sagittarians' arch-enemies?"

The Draconian's red eyes bulge. "Arch-enemies? You humans really are as stupid as you look. We were their loyal partners. Still are."

"Sure there's not much difference between partners and slaves," I mumble into my Budweiser. Big Tech has taught all us independent explorers that lesson.

"*They* were the Sagittarians' arch-enemies." The Draconi-

75

an flicks a claw at the solitary Silicon Person. "They drove us back all the way to the Core! We had to take refuge in here, with the only planet we had left! But as it turns out, hiding inside a supermassive black hole is a war-winning move. The Ggxkt'va went wild with victory, decided to upload themselves into the cloud, and well, you know what happened after that." It flicks its tongue disdainfully in the Silicon Person's direction, and saunters off on bare, clawed feet.

Finian leans back, rolling his can of Budweiser between his palms. He's been uncharacteristically quiet. I know why, too. He's sitting across from me, with the Sagittarian in his line of sight, and I've seen that look on his face before: on board the *Hellraiser*, for example, just before he knifed the Cannibal Captain. I feel a shiver of unease.

But even Finian is not idjit enough to start trouble here. I put that worry out of my mind and lean towards Sam. "I bet I know where they keep the good stuff," I whisper.

He's hunched over his Bud, biting his lips.

"Sam! I know where the A-tech'll be. I worked as a nursing assistant for a couple of years." I take the glazed look in his eyes for surprise. I agree, it does sound out of character for me. I only did it to earn a few quid while Donal and I were building the *Skint Idjit*, because my dad threatened to kick me out of the house unless I got a job. "The old dears all kept their valuables in their rooms. They'd be swearing me to secrecy and slitting open the mattress to show me their collection of rare euro coins. Mementoes from the Turkish civil war and so forth." No, I did not steal any of their little treasures. I have got some self-respect. At least, I had in those days.

The stuff was mostly worthless, anyway. But it'll be different here. "So we'll just have a ramble around, Sam, and if the lizard-faces ask awkward questions, we were just exploring."

He hasn't heard a word I've said.

"Sam?"

He bursts out, in a hoarse whisper: "I think my dad might be here."

CHAPTER 11

"My dad was an explorer," Sam says. We're outside the bar, walking down the main street, between buildings that only Hitler could love. Finian's with us. He listens with furrowed brows to Sam's story. "His name was Owen Slaughtermore. My mom met him on Cygnus 2c when he tried to jump her claim. I guess it was a hate-at-first-sight thing, and then they hooked up." Sam spreads his hands, as if to acknowledge that it's a puzzling scenario. It's not at all puzzling to me. "He stuck around until I was about a year old. Then he vamoosed. My mom was pissed as hell."

That is not puzzling, either. Not if you know Special Delivery Sam. I know her by reputation only, but Finian nods. "I remember she mentioned him to me. *Not* in the most flattering terms." He leans close to me and whispers, "His name was not Slaughtermore. It was Jones."

Sam walks on, hands in his pockets. "A guy called Slaughtermore, he should have a rep, right? But I never heard anything about him while I was growing up. It was a mystery. When I got to be eighteen or so, I asked my mom point blank if she knew where he was. And she said, 'You're shit out of luck, bud. He boarded the Ghost Train.'"

I hesitate. "But why do you think he's *here*, Sam?" It seems to me much more likely that Owen Jones got off at Merrielande, or one of the Ghost Train's other regular stops, assuming he was a halfway decent explorer.

"Because Caleb said so!"

"When did he say that?" Finian asks sharply.

"A couple of days ago. I was bugging him about this supposed train station. And he said there are some humans here. Like homeless people living in Grand Central, he said. I dunno about Grand Central, but that has to be my dad." Sam gives us an anguished grin. "He was the kind of guy who could survive anywhere."

This still doesn't prove anything to me, but I can read the tension on Sam's face. He won't leave here without trying to find his father.

Finian sighs. "Sorry, Sam. I'm having nothing to do with it."

"I couldn't do anything to help my mom," Sam says. "But maybe I can help my dad. I have to at least try."

"I'd like to show them we humans are not as stupid as they think we are." Finian gives a twisted smile. "That's a good way to prove the opposite."

"If I don't at least try to find him, I won't be able to look myself in the face," Sam mutters.

I draw a deep breath. "OK, Sam. I'll help you look for him."

His face lights up. "You're the best, dude!"

I feel a bit bad now. "I don't think we'll find him, mind you."

"I just want to try."

Finian shakes his head. "Just make sure you're back in time for the pub quiz."

"Pub quiz?" I say, mystified.

"Yeah, there was a sign on the notice-board as we came in. Did you not see it?"

"I didn't even notice the notice-board."

Finian smiles sourly. "I notice everything. It was one of those multilingual signs. It said there's a pub quiz at thirteen o'clock tonight. Now, I don't know how they count time here ..."

"Is it anything to do with us, though?"

"I have a feeling it is," Finian says. "I'm going to see if I can get anything out of Caleb about it, but I've got a feeling it could be important."

"I suppose maybe we're good for one thing, and that's entertainment value," I say.

"Something like that. Anyway, I want all of us there. I'm assuming it's after dark, so get back by sundown, and you should be all right."

"Will do," Sam says, champing at the bit.

Finian trudges back towards the Nursing Home at the Core the Galaxy, and Sam and I split up to search the city for his dad.

At least that is what *he* thinks we are doing.

Wandering along a street as wide as a motorway, which is probably a Sagittarian alley, I gaze up at the horned towers stabbing the sky. It's a dull sky, the color of an ocean covered by a petroleum slick. The Sagittarians transported this planet inside a supermassive black hole, complete with its star, and its atmosphere and everything. They *moved* a *star!* And they've kept this place ticking over for a *billion* years, give or take. I can't even begin to conceive of the technology you'd need for that.

I do know I want it.

This is the find I've been dreaming of all my life.

The level of A-tech we're talking about here, just one little sample would do me. Something small and portable.

Something I could use to foil the gandy dancers, hijack the Ghost Train, and return in triumph to dear distant Earth.

And I realize this may be exactly how Owen Jones *(if* he's here) ended up trapped on Pron, but I really don't think he's here. Putting myself in his shoes, I'd be storming the Ghost Train right now, begging to be let back on board. But he's not done that, and he's had multiple chances over the last quarter-century, and he's never done it.

The city is dead quiet, my own footsteps the only sound to be heard.

"Jones!" I halloo. "I mean Slaughtermore! Are you here?"

I'll keep this up for a little while, so I can tell Sam I tried. Then I'll double back and nose around the Nursing Home at the Core of the Galaxy. That'll be where the good stuff is. I bet I can get around those Draconians.

"Slaughtermore!"

The dead air swallows my voice.

I reach a crossroads. In both directions, empty, dusty motorways stretch into the distance. The buildings on the cross street have pediments supported by fifty-foot statues of the Manager, or his hairy cousins. The statues' eyes seem to burn into me the way the real Sagittarian's did.

Right. I've had enough of this.

I turn on my heel—and freeze.

The Silicon Person from the bar is floating in the middle of the street behind me, utterly silent on its gravsled.

I assume it's the same one from the bar, anyway. It's a shiny black pyramid about seven feet high, coated in overlapping tiles like the hide of an armadillo. Every angle and corner glitters as if machined by a nanoscale cutting tool.

I start to sidle around it, back the way I came. The tiles near the top flutter up and down minutely. Jesus, this has to be the spookiest of all the aliens.

I stop as a thought strikes me. Before I can change my mind, I say, "Silicon Person? Have you ever seen any others like me around here?"

"Carbon-based beings?" Its voice is unexpectedly mellifluous, and yet mechanical. After all, it's a silicon-based being. It hasn't even got lungs.

"Well, I was specifically thinking of human beings. You know, about this tall, two legs, two arms."

"There is another one like you over there." A tile sharpens to a point to indicate Sam's approximate location. "And two more in the community lounge."

"Yeah, I know about them. This one would have been here longer. He's … erm … Welsh-looking. At a guess."

After a pause, the Silicon Person says, "There is an animal husbandry and crop production area outside the city. It provides calories in carbon-based format. Some of your kind work there. I cannot say if any of them are Welsh-looking."

"Oh!" That's promising. Sam will be off to this 'animal husbandry and crop production area' like a shot.

"Is there anything else you seek?"

I hesitate. "The meaning of life?"

"I am afraid billions of years of life have made me no

wiser in that regard."

"That's all right. Everyone knows it's 42, anyway." I snicker to myself. The joke escapes the Silicon Person, as well it might.

"I know a great many other things," the Silicon Person offers. "Would you like to know how to reconcile quantum mechanics with general relativity?"

"Erm … Hasn't general relativity sort of been blown out of the water already? I mean, the Railroad …"

"I could explain how the Railroad utilizes the M-field to eliminate relativistic time dilation," the Silicon Person says eagerly.

I hold up my hands. "Jesus, please no. My head's an inch from exploding already."

The Silicon Person draws back.

"Sorry," I apologize. "The truth is I'm shite with equations. You know, we're beings of mediocre intelligence. Not enough brainpower to process that kind of thing. I'm sure it's very interesting, though."

The Silicon Person's lower tiles rise a couple of inches and then fall again. I interpret this for some reason as a sigh. Suddenly it dawns on me: the Silicon Person is very old, and it just wants to talk. It was the same at the nursing home in Ennis. You *could* do the minimum, change their bedpan, get them dressed, bring them a cup of tea, the end. But that's inhuman. They're human beings and you should treat them like human beings. So I'd always spend a few minutes (or a few hours) chatting with the old dears, and I ended up losing the job because my productivity wasn't meeting the shitehead manager's target.

"Do you like it here, then?" I say, as if I were sitting beside the Silicon Person's bed with a cuppa and a Hob Nob.

"I hate it," says the Silicon Person.

Well, that's refreshing. At the nursing home, it would be, "Sure love, I'm grand," and then a few months later they'd pop off from sheer despair.

"I am the last of my kind," the Silicon Person goes on, "and I am doomed to spend eternity as a prisoner of the Manager, so that he can glory eternally in the Ggxkt'va's downfall, and remind me every day that the Sagittarians conquered the galaxy."

"Well, hang on. The Sagittarians haven't conquered the galaxy. He's the last of *his* kind, too."

"Yes," says the Silicon Person, "but he controls the Railroad. Who controls the Railroad, controls the galaxy. That must be obvious ..." Even to you, remains unspoken.

"I see your point all right," I say, and I do.

To think we humans prided ourselves on being masters of the universe. To think of the way we've rampaged around in our pathetic little nuclear-powered spaceships, picking up this and that and saying "Hmmm, wonder how this works?"

And all the time, the Manager was sitting in the core of the galaxy, hearing reports from his gandy dancers, I've no doubt, and getting endless entertainment out of our stumbles.

"So what does he think of us?" I say, with no very high hopes. "I mean, we've been zooming around on the Railroad that his folk built ..."

"He *says* the Sagittarians built it, but in fact it was mostly Draconian labor."

"Somehow I'm not surprised. But does he think ... I

mean, I don't know … does he think we're worthy successors to the Sagittarian Empire?"

I am expecting the answer to this to be a resounding NO, and so I'm surprised when the Silicon Person lifts the tiles on one side of its body, then the other side, in an approximation of a shrug. "He has not yet made up his mind."

"Eh? He's had forty-three years to think about it!"

The Silicon Person's tiles all ruffle at once, making a sound like a fistful of coins dropped on the floor. "Please recall how old we are." The bugger's laughing at me. "Please think of forty-three human years in this context."

"Ah … right."

"It took him one hundred and twenty human year-equivalents to make up his mind about the Pygmy Ents."

A cold foreboding clutches my gut.

"And what was his decision regarding them?" I ask, although I already know.

"They were not deemed management material," the Silicon Person says. Its mechanical voice seems to soften a bit. "They were destroyed. I did not witness it myself, of course, but I am assured the process was humane."

I know better. I've seen pictures of the Pygmy Ents' home planet. It looks like fecking Pompeii. The scientists rub their chins and go "natural disaster," and the explorers nod wisely and say "war of planetary reduction," and the greens go "look, look, this is why nuclear power is evil," and oddly they're the ones who came closest to being right, aren't they? Because the Silicon Person's just told me what really happened to the Pygmy Ents.

They were nuked from orbit.

And now I bet I know what's behind all those doors marked PRIVATE on the Ghost Train.

I clench my fists, gnawing on my lips, fighting sheer terror. Up until this moment I'd have said I don't give a feck about humanity. But it turns out I do. I visualize Lisdoonvarna, my parents' house, the O'Learys' pile on the hill, O'Donoghue's pub, that field where I spent a drunken night as a fifth-year. I vividly picture everything going down in a sea of flames.

"Is there anything we can do to influence his decision?" I say "I mean, what does he consider to be management material?" I'd prefer to give the Manager a beating than pass his stupid test, but that is not on the cards, for the reasons already noted—technological gap, enormousness of.

"That I am not sure of," says the Silicon Person. "But you can and must influence his decision. That is what you are here for."

"Eh?"

"You must win the Pub Quiz tonight."

CHAPTER 12

"I met a Denebite," says Sam, bursting with his news. "She just came up to me and we got talking. It was really interesting! She offered to tell me about quasar formation and the Big Crunch. I was like, uh, sorry, I suck at that stuff." He chortles.

"Yeah, me too," I say, thinking of my own chat with the Silicon Person.

It is enough to make you weep, when you think of the human beings who have taken the Pub Quiz previously, as supposedly representative members of our species:

- Daredevil explorers—Owen Jones and others like him, of whom the less said the better
- American fighter pilots (yes, of course, humanity's initial reaction to the Ghost Train was to try to shoot it down; that cannot have impressed the Manager, although I hope the flyboys made a good showing in the physics section of the Pub Quiz)
- Russian fighter pilots
- Chinese fighter pilots
- French fighter pilots (what on earth did they *think*

would happen?)

- The passengers of that interstellar cruise ship that took off at the wrong time from Treetop fifteen years ago

Not a scientist among them, not a Nobel Prize winner, not even an engineer. The cruise ship, worse luck, was filled with tourists, not residents of Treetop. Stackers don't go on cruises.

- And now it is the turn of a handful of hapless A-tech thieves—ourselves.

"Your Denebite," I tell Sam, "was trying to help you cram for the Pub Quiz. I suppose they don't want to see another intelligent species go down in flames. I had the Silicon Person do the same thing to me. Talk about pushing water uphill. "

"Well, I told her I don't give a hoot about the Pub Quiz, and I don't give a hoot about Earth, either," says this heartless youth. "I mean, I come from Omega Centauri."

"Think the Manager would overlook our colonies when he gives the planetary reduction command? Think again."

"Well, you could be right. But there's nothing we can do about that. And maybe I *can* do something for my father."

Jesus, yes, the animal husbandry and whatever it was area. I forgot about that.

Before I can open my mouth to warn Sam off, he goes on, "I asked the Denebite! She said there are about fifty human beings here, working on, get this, a *farm!*"

"Did she say what they did to deserve that?"

"Oh, they took the Pub Quiz, and lost. So the Manager enslaved them," Sam says, with remarkably little feeling. I recall that his mother treated her defeated enemies in much the same way. Then his mouth squares and his eyebrows crinkle for a moment. He's not unfeeling. He's just barely holding it together. "The Denebite told me where the farm is. I have to go and see … if there's anything I can do for my father…"

I never heard of such a futile gambit, but I suspect he just wants to see the man, maybe touch his hand through the barbed wire.

"All right, away you go."

He wouldn't be any use in the Pub Quiz, anyway. He never went to school at all.

He lopes off down the street. Long shadows have slid in from the west. Pron's lonely sun is setting.

I head back towards the gate, thinking that I'll be no use in the Quiz, either. Could I decline to participate? You *can*, the Silicon Person told me, when I pressed it for more information. That's what Caleb did. That's why he's still travelling around the galaxy instead of husbanding animals on Pron. He's been un-personned. Now he gets to drink rum and cokes for all eternity, instead of worrying about the fate of Earth.

Finian comes out of the Nursing Home building. He waves urgently to me. I jog to meet him.

"Listen, Finian, I've heard about this Pub Quiz. You were right. It's the most important thing any of us will ever do. But I'm thinking I'd be no bloody good at it. I'm rubbish at maths and science …"

"Of course you are," my uncle snaps. "So it's a good job we've got someone else who isn't. Go and get Imogen!"

"Imogen?"

"Yes, Imogen!" He glances at the fading light. "It turns

out they've got twenty-seven hours in their day. Thirteen o'clock is in about forty minutes. Hurry up!"

I balk. I had a different errand in mind. The Silicon Person told me some other things after it finished telling me about the Pub Quiz. I did not mention these things to Sam. Have you ever wondered why I have no mates? Wonder no more.

"Why Imogen? I mean, she's got a good head on her, but …"

"Idjit! She's a stacker!"

Imogen?

A stacker?

Alternately jogging and walking back to the Ghost Train, I consider this amazing assertion. And actually, it's not so amazing. Once I get over being gobsmacked, the pieces all fall into place.

Inside the Ghost Train, I pay a quick visit to the Wonder Wall. Then I leg it back to the parking bay. The setting sun shines through the transparent walls. Shadows pool beneath the parked spaceships and cars.

I knock on the window of the police cruiser. "Imogen. Imogen. I need to talk to you."

"Go away."

The door's not locked. I take off the rucksack I had the Wonder Wall make for me, and climb into the back.

It is nice and peaceful in here. I can see why she doesn't want to budge. Even the faint rank smell you get when a vehicle's been slept in is not unpleasant. It's the spaceship smell I've lived with half my life. She's a lump in the corner of the back, hidden under the velour blanket she got from the Wonder Wall. I lay a hand on the bulge I take to be her hip. "I know you're a stacker, Imogen."

Silence.

"You came out to Arcadia to work for Samsung … as a reverse-engineer. You mentioned that when we first met. I should have put two and two together. I mean, I've never met a reverse-engineer who isn't a stacker. But …"

Her head pops out of the blanket. "But it didn't make sense to you that a stacker would be drinking by herself in the Pravda, so you figured they must have fired me for not making the grade."

"Yeah."

"Well, they didn't. They fired me for not being a team player. But by the time we met, I'd already stopped taking the drugs. And boy oh boy, you lose your edge fast if you don't take the drugs. I mean, I had the prebirth IQ optimization. My DNA is so tweaked, it looks like Frankenstein's monster. I had early childhood enrichment, afterschool classes, the works. I graduated cum laude from Princeton. But it's the nootropics that really put the cherry on the pie." She turns to me, and in the dimness, she looks just the way she did when I first laid eyes on her at Pravda. "When I couldn't afford the nootropics anymore, I found out what it was like to be ordinary. And I got to like it. Fletch, it's *exhausting* to be a stacker. Knowing you're different from everyone else. There's this gap between you and everyone … everyone. You know they're looking at you. Judging you. Othering you, and fetishizing you at the same time. I guess you wouldn't understand. The only way I can put it is it made me so *tired* … "

Yes, she is a stacker all right. It's the self-pity that confirms it. It reminds me of Ruby. And of myself at times, but that's a different story. I let my hand fall away from her hip.

"So I told Finian," she says, "that if there was anything I could do …"

"When was this?"

She purses her lips. "Right after we got here. When the gandy dancers called us beings of mediocre intelligence."

I remember that bland judgment. It pissed me the feck off, too, and I couldn't even take issue with its factual correctness.

"I realized, holy shit, they've made up their minds about us, but they're basing that on people like *Caleb*. Think about it. Back in the 20th century, who did they abduct? Rednecks driving home on country roads. Obese mothers of five. Counterculture cranks who'd pickled their brains with LSD."

See what I mean? The condescension is breathtaking. But I say nothing. If Finian could take it, so can I.

"So the gandy dancers have us pegged as low-IQ monkeys. But that was before we started using A-tech for DNA optimization. The nootropics are A-tech-based, too." She bites her nails. "I've been taking the whole stack for two weeks now. Finian's been getting them out of the Wonder Wall for me, so the gandy dancers don't guess."

"What was the plan?"

"Oh, we thought I might be able to take over the Ghost Train." She laughs bitterly. "That was before the whole supermassive black hole thing. At this point I'm like, um, yeah. Humanity is pretty much fucked."

"Not yet, it isn't," I say. "Come on."

I twitch her blanket away. As I expected, she's clutching her iPhone. She's also in her pyjamas.

"Get dressed," I tell her. "And bring your iPhone."

Even I, an ordinary non-optimized human being, can put two and two together and get four, sometimes.

On our way to the Nursing Home at the Core of the Galaxy, I rapidly fill Imogen in about the Pub Quiz. By the time we reach the community lounge, it's starting.

The Draconians are pushing the tables into groups in front of the television. The screen flickers through a multi-lingual announcement ending in the English words: THE GREAT PRON PUB QUIZ. Each species has congregated at its own group of tables. Excited hums, clicks, whirrs, and chirrups enliven the atmosphere. It looks as if everyone's taking part:

- Five Klingons
- Seven Denebites
- Four Puzzlers
- Sixteen Yellows (bright yellow, hermaphroditic, three-foot-tall dwarfs)
- Three Krells
- An indeterminate number of Draconians (they keep popping up and down, so it's not clear how many of them are actually playing)
- One Silicon Person
- And one Sagittarian.

The Manager has brought his throne down into the midst of his captive court. He's got a feast heaped on a special high table in front of him. Roast meat, a bucket full of soup, greens piled up like grass cuttings. I can smell it from here. The slaves are doing a yeoman's job on that farm.

The Manager turns his goatish face to us and draws back his lips in a snarl.. Then he picks up a roast haunch of Christ-knows-what, and tears into it with his yellow chompers, staring at us all the while.

"Oh God," Imogen says. "I can't do this."

"You can do it." I drag her to the table where Finian is sitting by himself. "Finian. Finian. Can she use her iPhone?"

"Is it against the rules, you mean? I don't know. Ask *him.*"

I edge towards the Manager. The food on his high table smells good at first, but then the smell coming off the Manager himself makes me want to throw up. The animal part of my brain tells me to run in the other direction and keep going. "Sir. Can we use a calculator?"

"You may use an entire set of the Encyclopaedia Brittanica if you want." He's got a high singsong voice, like a goat's *maaaaa.* He suddenly reminds me of the head teacher at Lisdoonvarna Secondary School. "Your defeat is certain, anyway."

Which is exactly the tone my old head teacher would take when he prophesied that I was destined for prison or an early grave, and it's looking like that was an uncommonly good prediction. But where there's life, there's hope. "Thank you very much, sir," I say, sucking up. You have to suck up to these little Hitlers. It's what they live for.

Back at our table, Finian is terrifying Imogen by telling her that the fate of humanity depends on her performance. Apparently, this is humanity's 38th Pub Quiz and we haven't won a single one yet. Even the Pygmy Ents had won a couple of times by this point.

I break in: "It's OK, Imogen. You can use your iPhone."

"Oh, thank God," Imogen gasps. Finian looks puzzled. He was not in that flying saucer with us.

I give Imogen the ghost of a wink. "And now I'll be off."

"No! You have to stay! Please, Fletch!"

"I'd only distract you," I say.

"Let the skiving wee cunt go," Finian says. He thinks I'm saving my own skin at the expense of our species. Taking the Caleb option.

But I never did really hit it off with Caleb, despite our superficial similarities.

He's missed so many tricks! He's been around the Railroad how many times, visited Pron how many times? And there he is now, sat in the corner of the bar, comfortably out of the action, enjoying his biannual rum and Coke. A lack of vision to see the possibilities, that's his problem.

As I turn to leave the bar, the first question flashes up on the television screen. I pause to read it.

Explain the theory of convergent evolution, providing at least three examples.

Oh, that's an easy one. Even I could answer that. Convergent evolution is what happens when God keeps bollixing it up, and trying the same thing again with variations, determined by all that's holy to get it right *this* time.

But that's probably not the answer the Manager is looking for.

I leave Imogen writing furiously on her answer pad, and wander out into the dusty, now-dark foyer of the Nursing Home at the Core of the Galaxy.

The alien babble fades behind me as the door of the bar swings shut.

On one level, any nursing home that's got a bar in it can't be all bad.

Even if it only serves Budweiser and cocktails.

But as I know from my brief, inglorious time working at Shadylawns in Ennis, visitors never see the ugly bits. They don't see the residents with dementia stuck upstairs. They don't see the minimum-wage assistants (such as yours truly) stripping twenty beds a day and hauling the shit-stained sheets down to the laundry truck. They don't see the nurses sitting on the back steps, smoking a fag so they won't break down in tears today. No matter how much technology advances, there'll still be jobs that only sapient beings can do, while loathing every minute of it.

So I'm not surprised when our Draconian waiter sidles out of the bar, scans the shadows for me, and then meanders in my direction, while pretending to polish the pillars with a grubby towel.

When it gets close enough, it gives a fake start of surprise. "Oh, it's just one of the ape-faces."

I point towards the street. "There's an escape in progress at the farm. You'd better send some of your lads to deal with it."

This is why I have no friends.

"Thanks for the tip," says the Draconian. It opens its mouth and gapes with all its teeth showing. The teeth gleam in the thin starlight from outside. I take this unpleasant sight for a smile.

"It's great the way you turn out the security forces at the first sign of any threat to the Manager," I say admiringly.

Its tongue flicks out and back. "Oh, you know us Draconians. Fanatically loyal. Impeccable work ethic. *No* objection to getting gunned down by the million in an asinine war between two equally arrogant and bloodyminded empires."

"And not in the least bothered about it, umpty million years later."

"One billion, three hundred and fifty six million years.

One billion, three hundred and fifty six million years."

"That's a long time."

"Time flies when you're having fun." Flick, flick, goes the tongue. The Draconian swipes its dustrag over another pillar. The pillar is decorated with a carving of the Manager. It is possible to dust with extreme prejudice. I've seen it.

"I bet you'd be having even more fun," I say, "if you hadn't been bereaved of your ancestral talismans."

This was the tip the Silicon Person gave me. The ancient being intimated that these ancestral talismans, whatever they may be, represent the dark side of Draconian warrior culture. The Manager saw fit to take them off the Draconians and lock them up. I can see his logic. But I am not on *his* side.

"Sss!" The Draconian rises onto the balls of its clawed feet. A spiky ruff spreads from the nape of its neck, ripping through the collar of its polo shirt, giving it a dinosaur appearance. *"Sssss!!"* The hiss seems to stir the very dust in the ancient hall.

"All right, all right … you'll have security on top of us …"

"We *are* security."

And bloody useless you are, too, I think to myself. Go, Sam, go! "Yes, but even so, there are places you can't get to, aren't there?" That's what the Silicon Person said. "Things you can't get *at …?"*

"Yes." The Draconian self-consciously smooths down its ruff, and tucks the spines back inside its collar. "Come on. I'll show you."

It leads me back into the bar. Question No. 3: *Estimate the number of surviving Population II stars in the universe.* Imogen's scribbling, glancing at her iPhone. She seems confident. The scoreboard above the television shows that all teams are tied at 20 points, except for the Yellows, who messed up on Question No. 2: *Explain why stature is a reliable indicator of mean intelligence in sapients.*

A crowd of decrepit residents has gathered to watch the Quiz, bobbling on their mobility chairs and having their drool wiped away by Draconian attendants.

My Draconian pal leads me around the fringe of the crowd, to the bogs.

"There," it says, pointing down.

CHAPTER 13

No. Ah, no.

I have taken many unpleasant journeys in my time but I had hoped to go to my grave without ever taking a journey head-first down a Sagittarian toilet.

Not that there is, in fact, a toilet in the lavatorial facilities of the Nursing Home at the Core of the Galaxy.

There's just a bright room with a stinking pond of sewage in the middle, fed by channels of fresh water from the walls. You're meant to squat over the channels. I'm basing that guess on the elephant-size turds stuck in one of them.

"Down there," says the Draconian, its red eyes rolling. It points into the pool. "Shaft, U-bend, cistern. Our talismans are in the cistern. We can't fit through the shaft. We've tried. No good."

"So there *are* disadvantages to being eight-foot warriors with the shoulder span of a rhino."

"Hurry up, ape-face, before someone comes in."

"Why don't you get the Yellows to do it?" They are only three feet tall.

"They can't swim."

"Neither can I," I lie half-heartedly.

"Are you going to do it or not?"

"No," I say, unlacing my Timberlands. "Not on your life," and I'm taking off my utility belt, transferring just two items to my pockets. "Under no circumstances," and I'm rewarded with a Draconian grin as I dip one toe into the reeking pool. If that turns out to have been my last sight in this life, I'll have paid for my sins before I reach purgatory.

"How would I get out again?" I say, just out of curiosity. "Swim back up?"

"Getting in is the hard part. Getting out is easy."

"How far down is—"

I do not get to finish the sentence. I barely even get to take a deep breath.

The Draconian leans over and gives me a big push.

I belly-flop into the reeking sludge. Ah God! My head's going under!

And I'm being sucked down, down, down. There's some kind of suction in the shaft. A flushing mechanism. My back scrapes stone, hard enough to take the skin off.

I flip, kicking frantically, so I'm swimming head-first. If that reptilian bastard was telling the truth, I've got to swim around a U-bend and then—

My head ploughs into something mushy. Frantically, I feel around with the hand that isn't pinching my nose shut. My fingers sink into what must be a year's build-up of alien turds. The waste is trapped, as I am, on this side of a metal grille that blocks the shaft.

I'm going to murder that Draconian, if it's the last thing I ever do—

Steady. Steady, Fletch.

I reach for the item I transferred to my left hip pocket. It's a miracle I don't cut my balls off getting it out.

An experienced A-tech scout never goes anywhere without his knife.

Or, as the case may be, someone else's knife.

And this one's metalforma.

Cuts through *anything*.

Eyes tight closed, lungs bursting, I hack at the grille.

Whoosh! The suction drags me, and all the solid waste, downwards. The edges of the hole I sawed in the grille snag my clothes and tear my skin. I kick madly. My tormented inner ear tells me I'm now swimming up.

I burst through the surface, gasping.

For a minute I tread water limply, revelling in the joy of breathing.

The smell of sewage is gone now. It's pitch-dark, but I get the sense that there's space around me, a roof above me.

An experienced A-tech scout never goes anywhere without a torch.

I wrestle mine out of my pocket and shine it around, dazzling myself until my eyes adjust.

Oh.

Stone pillars rise from the water and spread like trees to form arches supporting the roof. The water lapping at the pillars over the millennia has worn waists in the stone.

When lizard-face said a *cistern,* I was picturing an arrangement with a giant stopcock and ball valve. Many's the homeowner who tapes their valuables to the underside of a cistern lid in a waterproof bag. The Manager might have done the same thing with the Draconians' talismans.

But of course, there's this kind of cistern as well. A gigantic roofed reservoir.

Shining my torch down the water-floored avenues of columns, I am thinking more about finding the way out than finding the Draconians' ancestral treasures. There's an island over there! I swim towards it. My splashes echo under the roof. I drag myself out on the rocky edge of a platform heaped with boxes and containers.

Maybe this is where the Draconians' ancestral talismans are.

But how am I supposed to know what's what? I can't read alien squiggles.

All these boxes probably contain treasures of inestimable value. The crown jewels of a dozen interstellar empires.

I clamber over the boxes, towards the middle of the island—and as it turns out, I have no trouble identifying the Draconian talismans at all.

A smile spreads over my face.

It's a shame I can't take all of them. But I think I can manage three or four in each hand … no, but then I won't be able to swim … all right, let's try putting them in the old cargo pockets …and some down my t-shirt … and I can put some more down my Carhartts, and tuck my kecks into my socks so they don't fall out … and that's the lot! Grand.

Now I've just got to find the way out.

The Draconian was vague about that part. It just said getting out would be easy, compared to getting in.

In the middle of the island I find a machine that reminds me of the Wonder Wall on the Ghost Train: white buttons on white. My fingers itch. I'd kill for a Pepsi right now, flat or not. But randomly pushing buttons on a machine of unknown purpose really might qualify me for the Darwin

Awards. For once, prudence gets the better of curiosity.

I walk around the edge of the island, hoping for a boat. Instead, I find a causeway submerged a few inches beneath the surface of the water. I only know it's there because the water ripples differently above it. I step down onto the hidden surface. Jesus, it's slippery!

Slithering in my sock feet, I edge away from the island. After falling on my arse for the second time, I resort to crawling on hands and knees. The Draconian talismans drag down the front of my t-shirt and clank inside my trousers. Fatigue sets in by degrees. Shining my torch back the way I came, I can't believe I've only crawled thirty yards.

Suddenly, light shoots over the water ahead of me.

A door in the wall of the cistern!

I'm nearly at the end of this!

Hope dies when the light is blocked by the hulking silhouette of the Manager.

Oh Christ, I'm done for now. There were silent alarms. Of course there were. Why would the Manager have less security than King Zuckerberg of Treetop? Or maybe the Draconian squealed on me.

The Manager splashes out onto the causeway. He's got his own torch, a headlight-strength beam, fifteen feet up.

I slide down onto my belly and roll off the edge of the causeway.

The treasures in my clothes drag me down.

I clutch the edge of the causeway with my fingers, keeping my head just above water as the Manager stalks closer.

I can smell him now.

He's muttering to himself in Sagittarian. *Maaa, maaaa, maaaa.*

His torch beam zips towards me, and I duck my head under the water. If only the ripples don't give me away—

Ow! My fingers!

He's trod on my *fingers!*

But his next stride carries him past me, and by the time I surface in the wake of his footsteps, he's halfway to the island.

My *fingers!* The last three fingers on my left hand feel like they've been sliced off.

It could be worse.

I'm right-handed.

But Christ, the *pain* …

One-handed, I drag myself back onto the causeway. As fast as I dare, I shuffle towards the door the Manager left ajar behind him.

He's on the island now, muttering away. Asking a question, it sounds like. Maybe he's operating that Wonder Wall machine. Maybe he doesn't even know I'm here!

I crawl up the steps up to the door. Staying low, so he won't spot my shadow, I flop across the threshold. The door is twenty-five feet high and must weigh several tons. I'm violently tempted to slam it shut on him. But then he *would* know I'm here …

Where am I, anyway?

Furs, and bones, and heaps of straw litter the floor of a vast vaulted room.

This must be the Manager's bedroom! Goats like to sleep on straw, and I suppose omnivorous hyer-intelligent ones are no different. I gag at the putrid smell.

But the most extraordinary thing about this room is the walls.

They're covered with carvings, like most of the walls in this city. But these carvings do not depict Sagittarians. They show gandy dancers.

Thousands of them, all the way up to the ceiling, *on* the ceiling, all their little limbs tangled together, carved at different depths. Some are just the barest suggestion of domed heads. Others look like with a bit of encouragement, they might step straight out of the wall.

There's no accounting for taste, I suppose.

Clanking at every step, I hurry past the eerie carvings. It's a good thing the floor is covered with straw so my wet footprints don't show.

The door on the other side of the room leads to a dark hallway. I hear the noise of cheering from the bar. Thank God! I follow the sounds down a Sagittarian-sized stairway—jump, *clank*. Jump, *clank*.

I'm halfway down when a long-drawn *"Maaaaa!"* drifts from the darkness above me.

You hear about the howls of wolves, which used to be the most terrifying sound in the universe for our ancestors. I am here to tell you that not even the most ferocious canid could compete with the howl of a goat.

I jump down the rest of the stairs in a blind panic. At the bottom, the light of the bar television seeps under fringey hangings, and I know where I am.

I flatten myself against the wall.

The Manager strides past me, thrusting the hangings out of his way, and I get an instant's glimpse of the bar.

The hangings fall back. I lie down on my stomach—trying desperately not to clank—and crawl under the mossy folds of material, out onto the Manager's dais …

right underneath his throne.

He's not in it.

Peeking out from under the throne's heavy skirt of fur, I see that the crowd's closed in around the contestants. Only four teams are still in the game: the Denebites ... the Silicon Person ... and the Manager. He's back on his special bar stool, writing on his high table, the debris of his feast pushed aside.

The fourth surviving team is us.

The scoreboard reads:

Deneb: 140

Ggxkt'va: 170

THE EMPEROR OF THE MILKY WAY, THE UNIVERSE, AND EVERYTHING: 170

Earth: 170

Holy feck! Imogen is holding her own with the two most intelligent species in the history of the galaxy!

I'd cheer my throat raw, if I dared to make a sound.

I have to get off this fecking dais, but it's fifteen feet high and if I come out from under the throne, I'll be in full view.

The Draconians are all hanging around in the far corner by the entrance to the bogs. It's as if they think I'll be coming back that way.

I try to catch their eye, *without* catching the Manager's eye, but it's no good—they're all staring at the scoreboard, which is updating as the computer processes the contestants' answers to Question No. 25 *(Explain why the solipsistic philosophy fails, and summarize an argument that convincingly rebuts it).*

Deneb: 140

Ggxkt'va: 180

THE EMPEROR OF THE MILKY WAY, THE UNI-

VERSE, AND EVERYTHING: 180
Earth: 180

Ha, ha! So much for the Denebites' famed intelligence! Eat human dust, beak-faces!

With no realistic chance of winning, the Denebites withdraw from the quiz. It's just a trivial amusement to them, anyway. It makes no difference to *them* if they win or lose. *Their* home planet is already dead.

Ours isn't, but its fate hangs in the balance, and the tension escalates while the remaining teams wrestle with the next four questions. I forget that I'm lying under the Manager's throne with half a ton of hardware inside my sewage-soaked clothes. I almost forget to breathe. I'm riveted to the sight of Imogen bent over her answer pad. Her dark hair falls on either side of her face, exposing the white nape of her neck. She's so calm, she might as well be alone in the room. I'm reminded of the way she looks when she's piloting a ship. She makes it look effortless. Sometimes she looks things up on the iPhone.

Finian pretends to be helping her, but I think every sapient being can see it's her doing all the work.

Just as long as they don't guess it's actually the iPhone doing it.

Question No. 29: *Summarize the principles of imperialism and give the most common reasons for the collapse of empires.*

She refers to the iPhone repeatedly on this one.

The Silicon Person holds a stylus in one of the tentacles it can extrude from between its middle tiles. It completes its answer in a few seconds, puts down its stylus, and goes back to floating impassively on its gravsled.

The answers pop up on the screen. Imogen and the

Manager have both written essays, but the Silicon Person's answer is just two words long:

Fuck This.

Howls, chirrups, squeaks, and hisses of laughter rock the room.

The Manager cuts the mirth off with a glare. "The Ggxkt'van has withdrawn from the Quiz," he bleats in that awful piercing singsong.

The Silicon Person floats away through the crowd, and I can't suppress a smile. Who knows what is passing through its old mind? But I imagine it is experiencing satisfaction.

It has probably guessed that Imogen is on the verge of winning the Pub Quiz thanks to her iPhone, which absorbed the entire collective wisdom of the Ggxkt'van race during its moment of freefall above their ex-planet.

Broadband wireless data transfer capability, baby.

Petabytes of information.

Here comes Question No. 30—the last. If Imogen aces this one, and the Manager fails it, we'll have won. If the Manager answers correctly, too, I suppose it'll go to a tie-breaker. But when I see the question, I relax.

Define hubris, and explain the role it plays in Ovid's Metamorphoses, particularly with regard to the poet's mythologization of Julius Caesar.

We've won.

Imogen won't need the iPhone at all for this.

She starts scribbling joyfully.

The Manager scowls at the television. He's got the hump altogether.

I have a feeling—just a feeling—that he came up with the questions himself, and this one was meant to be the cruellest cut of all. He'd have expected us to be left in the dust by now, unable to answer even the simplest question about galactic formation or the theory and practice of managing interstellar empires. Then—a question about *human* culture! What, you can't even answer that? Off to the farm with you, while your intellectual superiors enjoy a chortle at your expense.

It is a fair bet that previous human participants in the Pub Quiz did not know Ovid from their left elbow.

But Imogen did her degree in classical literature. She's actually giggling as she writes.

The Manager's got no idea what to put. Ha! He probably just copied that question off some internet source trawled up by the Ghost Train.

He rises. Everyone flinches out of his way. He's striding towards the dais, his goatish lips working, and suddenly the truth dawns on me.

This'll be the *second* time he's left the bar during the Quiz.

I don't stop to think. I wriggle out from under the throne and stand up. "He's cheating!" I howl. "He's away upstairs to look up the answer on the computer! He had to look up the answer to that other question, too—the one about philosophy!"

Everyone except Imogen stares at me in shock.

The Manager's face—on a level with mine, since I'm stood on the dais—contorts into a snarl.

"Cheat!" I screech. "You're a cheating piece of shite and we're not having it, are we lads!"

The response from the crowd is muted. Oh, dear. They all knew he was cheating. They just weren't going to say anything.

The Manager strides forward. An enormous hand lashes out. I dodge, but he's faster. He seizes me around the middle. He's got nails like yellow shovels, hair on his hands and arms like a mangy black carpet. I'm petrified, sure he will literally rip me in half, but instead he hurls me across the bar.

Like a human cannonball, I sail over the resident aliens' heads …

… and twenty-five lightsabers cascade from their hiding-places inside my t-shirt and trousers.

CHAPTER 14

I'd no reason to suspect that the Draconians' ancestral talismans would turn out to be lightsabers. Well, except for one little thing: me and Finian found our lightsabers on the Draco spur. So I was hoping against hope. These overlaps sometimes turn out to be coincidences …

… and sometimes, they don't.

The Draconian waiters, busboys, and nursing aides scrabble on the floor, snatching up their ancestral weapons with hisses of joy.

And I crash head-first into the wall.

I come to on the floor, feeling like I've been run over by a lorry.

There is a terrible racket of alien argument, but to my surprise and disappointment, there is no pitched battle. The Draconians are just waving their lightsabers and yelling at the Manager, who towers over the mob, *maaa*ing deafeningly. I was expecting he'd be in pieces by this time. That reptilian scrote who pushed me down the toilet certainly seemed to be promising a uprising by the Nursing Home's staff.

Maybe the Draconians are not so hard as they let on. I

suppose you *would* lose your edge after 1,536,000.000 years as a janitor.

Which means it'll have to be the real hard men who handle this.

I try to stand up. Something in my left leg goes *crunch* and I sit down again. My breath comes in short, shallow pants.

Imogen shoves through the crowd to me. "Fuck you," she says, half laughing and half crying. "I was really grooving on that Ovid question."

I reach into my cargo pocket with my good hand and extract the last lightsaber, the only one that didn't fall out during my maiden flight. "Give this to Finian."

What? When I said 'hard men,' did you think I was including myself? Away with you. *Finian's* the one who's got the right stuff. Me, all I've got is three broken fingers and probably a broken leg.

Imogen slaps the lightsaber away. "He's already got one," she says. "Quick!" She tries to pull me to my feet, and drops me again when I howl in pain.

"I've busted my fecking leg!"

Imogen darts into the crowd and comes back towing a mobility chair.

Meanwhile, the alien baying has gotten louder. The Draconians are threatening the Manager and the Manager's threatening them back, I'd say. Everyone else is streaming towards the exits.

"Where'd you get this?" I gasp, heaving myself into the mobility chair.

"I tipped a bunch of Yellows out of it."

"Good girl."

With Imogen standing behind the seat—which is greasy,

and all over yellow dandruff—I take the chair up as high as it will go. There's Finian's white head in the middle of the reptilian mob.

I grip my lightsaber between my knees, trying to aim it at the Manager's head. While I am not one for battle, I've no objection to sniping from a safe distance. But these weapons are not meant to be used one-handed. The bright blue beam springs out—and slices through the Manager's throne, missing the gent himself altogether.

The Manager lets out an earsplitting bleat of fury.

And a horde of gandy dancers bursts through the hangings behind the throne, tearing them down and trampling them in their berserk charge at the Draconians.

Not all of the gandy dancers are full-sized. Some aren't even fully formed. They're the carvings from the walls in the Manager's bedroom.

Carvings? Self-assembling robots, or something like that. The whole city is probably made of nano-wotsits. Bloody hell.

These larval gandy dancers may be tripping over their own feet, but they're as vicious as wolverines. With sweeping gestures, they bowl the Draconians head over heels. It's the tractor-beam effect. Lightsaber beams swing wildly, inflicting more friendly damage than otherwise. I smell reptilian flesh cooking.

Finian, left in the middle of the room, drops to one knee and meets the gandy dancers alone, like a musketeer standing his ground against a cavalry charge. He slashes his lightsaber across the first wave, cutting about twenty of them in half. It's beautiful, and then they overrun him.

The Manager leans against the wall in the corner, laughing

his head off, at least that's what I think he's doing. It's hard to hear over the screams.

I shove the lightsaber into Imogen's hands and dive the mobility chair down to Finian. Imogen stabs at gandy dancer heads. I lean over and grab Finian's arm. He's dazed, but he's still got hold of his lightsaber. He clambers onto the chair, standing astride me, which means the chair now can't rise more than six inches off the floor. But this also makes it too heavy for these immature gandy dancers to toss around.

We careen around the bar like a team of warriors in a battle chariot, buffeted by tractor beams, me steering, Imogen and Finian mutilating all the gandy dancers they can reach.

The Draconians, heartened, throw themselves back into the fray.

The Manager's not laughing anymore.

"Get him!" I shriek. "Get the Manager, for feck's sake!"

"I am stabbing the shite out of him!" Finian bellows. "He's got body armor!"

Indeed, the air around the Manager glows faintly blue. He's got some kind of a shield that absorbs and dispels the energy of the lightsabers. With a sinking feeling, I remember the Butterfly-zillas of Suckass. They absorbed energy. We were going to sell them to the military for energy shields. The Sagittarians probably made them.

The optics behind the bar disintegrate in a cloud of glass shrapnel. More gandy dancers surge over the bar.

"Retreat!" Finian bellows, using the voice that carried over the mayhem on the *Bagged & Tagged*, ten kiloparsecs from here.

The Draconians do not need telling. But as I slew the mobility chair around, they stumble back from the door that leads out to the foyer.

Something else is coming in.

It's a platoon of ragged, sinewy, barefoot … humans,

"Sam!" I yell. "Over here!"

Sam's eyes roll. He's supporting an older fella who's got to be the unfortunate Owen Jones—he's the spitting image of Sam himself, except for the white hair. Sam's liberated the rest of the farm workers, too, and they've arrived just in the nick. I always said that boy had a superlative sense of timing.

The whole heap of them dive for cover, scattering like dead leaves in the tractor beams crisscrossing the bar.

Ah. They were not coming to our aid, after all.

They were fleeing ahead of …

An enormous hand closes on the jamb of the door, and rips the entire frame out of the wall.

The hand is identical to the Manager's, except it's pale gray.

So is the head that now pokes in through the crumbling opening.

It's one of the statues that used to support the buildings on the main street.

I *thought* I felt an earthquake a little while ago.

So the gandy dancers aren't the alpha and omega of the Manager's repertoire.

He can make anything he likes, can't he?

And what he likes is reflections of himself—

EMPEROR OF THE MILKY WAY, THE UNIVERSE, AND EVERYTHING—

—forever and ever.

The nano-stone Sagittarian head retreats. The hand

shoots back into the room up to the elbow, and seizes two farm workers. It drags them back out. Their screams cut off abruptly.

I lower the mobility chair to the floor. Imogen's clutching my shoulders. I squeeze one of her hands with my good one. "I'm sorry it didn't work in the end," I say.

Finian growls: "You give up too easily, Fletch."

He swings his leg across the handlebars and steps off the mobility chair. In a bowlegged stance like a boxer, he dances towards the door. His lightsaber beam leaps out and singes the knuckles of the giant hand that's now tearing out chunks of the wall, widening the opening.

I groan. He's decided to sell his life right now, right here … for *nothing*. I mean, it's not as if he can buy us time to get away. All he's doing is getting in a few kicks at THE EMPEROR OF THE MILKY WAY, THE UNIVERSE, AND EVERYTHING, for sheer spite. Because it's better than dying of cancer.

The Manager rights his bar stool and sits down amidst the carnage, savoring our destruction. When he sees Finian tickling his golem, he bleats in outrage. He gestures to his gandy dancers—

BLAM!

The Manager freezes, looking puzzled.

BLAM! BLAM! BLAM!

The Manager topples off his bar stool and plants his goatish face in the flood of spirits from the bar.

The gandy dancers sag in place. The golem stops tearing at the wall.

Black Sagittarian blood dribbles from the Manager's nose and mingles with the puddles on the floor.

A cackle fractures the silence. In the most distant corner of the bar, Caleb, whom I completely forgot about, slides off his stool. He saunters over to the corpse of the Manager and fires another round into his hairy ear.

"Just makin' sure." He blows on the muzzle of his 1911. "Guess all that target practice paid off, huh?"

CHAPTER 15

All the gandy dancers have irretrievably frozen up except for the ones on the Ghost Train. Dizzy, Pew Pew, and the white-coats say it is only a matter of time until they themselves crash, too. The Manager's nanites—the invisibly tiny machines that lived in his body, keeping him in youthful fettle—were quantumly entangled, or unified in the M-field, or something equally incomprehensible, with the nanostuff that's everywhere on Pron, which can become carvings, or gandy dancers, or weaponized caryatids.

When we ventured out of the bar, we found a whole queue of sixty-foot golems in the foyer, their great grey heads stooped beneath the high ceiling, their car-sized fists bunched.

He'd summoned every robot in the city to come and tear us to pieces.

Now they're just statues again, petrified where they stand, as useless as that duplicator from Seventh Heaven that stopped working after copying a few wristwatches.

No Manager, no nano-wizardry.

The city's in a fair old mess. Fallen masonry (at least it

looks like masonry) litters the streets.

And 129 (!) ancient alien residents of the Nursing Home at the Core of the Galaxy haven't had their breakfast, or had their beds changed, and the lavatory is blocked up, and the television is broken, which you'd think they would not be complaining about, but they are, they are. And there's no food coming from the farm anymore because all the surviving slaves are now ensconced on the Ghost Train. Like rabbits down a fecking hole. They're eating hamburgers and chips and taking long hot showers and they won't budge at gunpoint. Not that I can blame them.

"Why don't you come with us?" I ask the residents. I've got them together in the wide street in front of the Nursing Home, which is only partially blocked by golems. It's a bright sunny morning on Pron. Occasional tremors shake the ground as another building, deprived of its support pillars, collapses in the distance.

The ancient aliens chirrup, squeal, whirr, and grunt. Eventually the Silicon Person floats out of the crowd to speak for them all. "We are used to it here."

Translation: They are used to being waited on hand and foot.

And as luck would have it, the only aliens dead set on accompanying us back to the Milky Way are the Draconians.

I rub my hands over my face. I don't know what to do. I feel fate closing in on me like a shadow out of the cloudless sky. Fletch, you wanted to be the king of your own planet one day. Here's your chance. Stay here and be the Emperor of the Milky Way, the Universe, and Everything.

I could probably master the Wonder Wall machine upstairs, given time.

F. R. SAVAGE

And if I stayed here, I'd have all the time in the universe.

Someone needs to look after these poor old souls, anyway.

And who else is going to do it?

Rusty guitar chords drift down the street.

I whip around, and nearly fall out of my mobility chair.

Caleb strolls through the gate, cowboy hat pulled down low, strumming his guitar:

Yippy yi yay, oh yippy yi oh
Ghost riders in the sky

He breaks off and says with a twisted smile, "I lost my soul long ago, Fletch. Cain't get it back, no matter how many aliens I kill. So maybe it's time for me to help these old aliens stay alive." He shrugs. "I had enough of endless riding through the skies, anyway. I'll stay here."

"You can't do that."

"Cain't I? You jest watch me. Hey, Dggkchak?" He addresses the Silicon Person by a name I never knew it had. "We'll have us some games of canasta. Get a domino tournament going. No more goldurn Pub Quizzes. No more Sagittarian war videos, either. I got five thousand hours of downloads here—" he touches his wristwatch— "Seinfeld, the History Channel, the Simpsons. Y'all are gonna love this stuff."

"No," I says. "Caleb, the point is you can't make it work. Potatoes don't grow themselves. Who's going to hoe the fields while you're playing dominoes? Who's going to do the washing and cooking?"

"We are," Caleb says. "No more sittin' around on our behinds, ain't that right, guys?" He gets a few dubious chirrups. "Ya don't work, ya don't eat, that's the law of the universe. This's been a lawless place, but that is gonna change." The ancient aliens nod dubiously. "However, I appreciate that y'all are old and infirm. So Fletch, next time you swing by Earth, I would be greatly obliged if you get the word out to the Knights of Columbus and the Rotarians. I 'spect there'll be no shortage of volunteers."

"I can see it already," I say, giving in. "The Kibbutz at the Core of the Galaxy."

"Naw, uh uh, none of that Commie shit. Point is, I want charitable organizations involved from the get-go, so we ain't overrun by guys like you, trying to steal our shit." He slaps me on the shoulder. "Now you better git on back to the train. Finian's as sick as a three-legged dog."

I thought he looked a bit poorly last night.

But it's a death's-door scene that I find in the lounge. He's lying on the floor, surrounded by people who don't know what to do for him. What *do* you do when a legend collapses? His face is the color of recycled paper. The flesh of his cheeks has fallen in, leaving his cheekbones prominent. He's got so thin.

Imogen sits by his head, wringing her hands. "I think he's had a stroke. He won't tell me anything."

"I thought it was lung cancer," I say.

"It's everything," Finian croaks, "catching up with me at once. I'm seventy-six bloody years old. What do you expect?"

I tip myself off my mobility chair. My leg, in a makeshift splint, hits the ground badly. Finian hears my yelp and manages a thin smile.

"Get yourself some pain pills out of the Wonder Wall. That's all it's good for."

"You're going in one of those." I drag on his shoulder

with my good hand, pointing at the nearest couch.

"Feck off! You wouldn't go in, why do you want me to?"

"Because if you don't, you're going to die."

"So fecking what," he says, and closes his eyes.

"I won't let you die like this."

"Are you afraid I'll come back to haunt you? Heh, heh." His laugh turns into a racking cough. Imogen holds his shoulders.

"You're just scared."

"So are you."

"I'm scared of dying. *You're* scared of living."

There's nothing for it, then. I bend down and whisper into his ear, so quietly that no one else can hear.

Finian's eyes pop open. "Jesus," he says. "You make a good point, lad." He tries to push himself upright. "Get me on that bloody couch!"

So he vanishes inside a Tomb of Youth, and comes out hale and roaring, full of vim, just the way he was on the Draco spur when I first crewed for him, and I almost wish I hadn't persuaded him to have the rejuvenation treatment.

Almost.

Because, as I whispered into his ear while he lay dying, if he were dead, who'd drive the Ghost Train?

"WE REQUIRE A SAPIENT DECISION-MAKING AUTHORITY," Dizzy and Pew Pew told me after the battle. "WE WOULD RATHER HAVE IMOGEN. BUT SHE REFUSES. WE WILL SETTLE FOR YOU."

"Let me get this straight," I told them. I was in terrible pain at the time, the adrenaline all gone, my fingers and my leg throbbing fit to fall off. "You'd let me drive the Ghost Train? *Me?*"

"SAFEST PLACE FOR YOU."

I see now that they were trying to talk me out of staying on Pron. But at the time I just thought they were rubbing it in that everything I touch goes to shite. Oh, it's a dark place you go after there's been fighting and killing. Even victory feels like a personal failure, and all you want to do is take a handful of pills and dive into a bottle, and there aren't any bloody bottles left because they're all smashed on the floor, and the corpse of the Manager is sprawled in the shards. I had to organize some of the farm workers in the end to drag him down to the sea and tip him in. It was getting on for twenty-one o'clock by then and Pron's moon was up, very big and bright. We saw the nanites starting to flee from his body, like drops of mercury oozing out of his pelt, vanishing into the ground of Pron.

"You want to put that shite in me?" I said to Dizzy and Pew Pew. "Not in a billion years, am I making myself clear?"

"THEN THE GHOST TRAIN WILL NEVER MOVE AGAIN," they said, standing on the shore of the sea in their little baggy overalls. "ALSO, INTERSTELLAR RAIL-ROAD WILL NO LONGER BE MAINTAINED. TRACKS WILL BREAK. JUNCTIONS WILL BECOME ERRATIC …"

"You're threatening me with a strike."

"FOR BEING OF MEDIOCRE INTELLIGENCE, YOU ARE NOT STUPID."

I tore my hair a bit thinking about it. I was still down by the water, after sending the farm workers back to the Ghost Train. I sat on the shore of that alien ocean and lost my mind for a little while.

Eventually I said: "Would you take someone else, at all?"

I know, I know. It was a mean trick I played on them. They wanted better working conditions. They are now finding out what it's like to crew for Finian.

Video games and football on all the newly installed screens in the lounge, constant roars of "This is not satisfactory," Queens of the Stone Age and Eagles of Death Metal blaring from the newly installed speakers, and he's got the gandy dancers putting gold elephants on every bloody thing. He's going to round up all his old mates from the *Marauding Elephant* and recruit a cast of attractive young cabin attendants. Oh, and he's going to turn the parking bay into a mini Formula One race track. They will refurbish some of the more interesting alien vehicles to race with. He's got the Draconians working on that.

It's remarkable how well Finian gets along with the Draconians.

Remarkable to everyone who doesn't know him, that is.

Me, I'm content to just lie in my hammock and let time do its healing work on my broken bones and bashed-up flesh. I rigged my hammock on the observation deck to be as far as possible from the nonstop party at the other end of the Ghost Train. When I'm not too drunk, I watch the Milky Way reappear. We are shooting out of the core of Sagittarius A* on a jet of highly energetic particles, which coheres ahead of us into the familiar Railroad. Caleb was right—it's easier getting out than getting in—but it also takes longer. Almost a month passes before we reach the Norma arm, and then we're on the other side of the galaxy from Earth.

By this time I'm on my feet, able to eschew a mobility chair for an honest crutch. I kill time exploring the regions of the Ghost Train previously marked PRIVATE. Finian has done away with those restrictions. Nowhere is to be off-limits to humanity. Admittedly, no one ever goes down here, as there's not much to see—just a lot of computers, the same as in any spacecraft. The nukes are hidden away in their bomb bays and Finian is the only one who has access to them.

Still, Imogen finds it interesting down here. I meet her on the engineering deck, talking to one of the white-coated gandy dancers about the M-field and this and that.

"I won't have to work for Big Tech anymore," she says excitedly. "I'm going to start my own company."

"You're still taking the nootropic drugs, are you?"

She flushes. "Yes."

"Grand. Be all you can be, Imogen."

"Do you have a problem with that?" she shouts after me, as I swing away on my crutch. She's developed the ability to detect sarcasm, although I don't think the drugs helped with that. The opposite, if anything. It's just exposure.

"Not at all," I shrug.

It's my problem, not hers. My desire for her died when I found out she was a stacker. She doesn't understand that, and why should she?

She comes after me, pink with anger. "What are you going to do, Fletch?"

"Go back to the observation deck and have a drink. Only another four months until we get there."

Normally, it would have been two years, but Finian nixed the Ghost Train's traditional tour around the far side of the galaxy. It'll still be there next year, he said. So we are zooming back towards the Orion arm by the straightest route possible.

"That's what I mean," Imogen says, still following me. "What are you going to do when we get home?"

I can't answer that, because I don't know.

CHAPTER 16

"Land your craft immediately!"

An NEPD patrol ship buzzes me as I deorbit from the Railroad. Several more of them swarm out of Treetop's hazy atmosphere.

"Proceed to the coordinates I have provided! And no monkey business, or there won't be enough of you left to bury, hotshot!"

Here we go again, eh? These little Hitlers, never satisfied unless everyone is doing exactly as they say.

"Land your craft IMMEDIATELY!" the NEPD officer froths over the radio, incensed by the fact that I am not a stacker with lightning-fast reflexes, so it's going to take me a minute to alter my deorbit trajectory.

A patrol ship screams across my prow. It is needlenosed, painted in spiffy white and blue, a new addition to the NEPD's fleet. The department must be swimming in funds since our burglary of King Zuck's tree. Hard to believe that was eight months ago.

"Hey! Asshole!" the officer barks. "Proceed to the coordinates I have provided! You have five seconds! Five! Four!"

"OK, OK," I sigh into the radio, and follow them to a tree in the northern hemisphere.

It's one of the heavily-settled multi-owner ones, its canopy pimpled with spaceport terminals that sprawl over whole leaves. I set my ship down and wait.

The NEPD ships land in a cloud of rocket exhaust, boxing me in. The officers leap out and surround my ship. They have new uniform spacesuits, skintight, with pale blue Kevlar vests and codpieces.

"Do you know why I pulled you over?" the radio barks.

"Because I'm flying a refurbished Denebite star shuttle?"

"Shut up, smartass. You were wobbling all over the sky."

"I'm a shite pilot. Never claimed otherwise."

"Is that really a refurbished Denebite star shuttle?"

Out on the leaf's surface, the keener officers are targeting me with shoulder-mounted rocket launchers. I hope they're not thinking of using those. The canopies of Treetop trees are quite flammable.

A new voice booms into my cockpit. From the way the officers outside jump, I know they're hearing it, too. "Yes, it is a refurbished Denebite star shuttle! And if you saw it come off the Ghost Train, you're starting to catch on! The pilot is Fletcher Connolly. He is the only son of my own brother, and if you fuck with him, I will be very unhappy." The last words ooze out of the radio, hoarse with Irish menace. Even I shiver a bit. "You may ask why you should care if I'm unhappy. The answer is that I am the new chief of the NEPD! The name is Finian Connolly, and all of youse answer to me! I will be sorting out the details with your command structure on Earth shortly. For now, get rid of those awful uniforms you've got on. You look like faggots, the lot of you. And I'll be speaking to the idjit who issued you with rocket-launchers." *Click*.

I grin. "Thanks, Finian."

My comms screen displays a live video stream from the lounge-cum-bridge of the Ghost Train. Finian's crew of Draconians and liberated slaves are exclaiming over the views of Treetop. Finian's got his eye to the optic sight of the new broadside-oriented railgun he had the gandy dancers put in.

"I didn't say anything to them about the burglary," he remarks. "Want me to mention that?"

I think about it. "Nah, on the whole. We picked up nothing on the news, so hopefully they've forgotten about it."

"If they haven't yet, they will soon," Finian smirks. "I'll be getting off the air now. There's a heap of these bastards sniffing at my arse. I'm going to put a rod from God across their noses, so they know who they're dealing with. Connolly out."

"Connolly out," I echo, and turn off the radio.

I slide into my new spacesuit—a deliberately drab product of the Wonder Wall—and deplane with a smile on my face.

My good mood curdles when I have to pay four figures for a taxi to Wilkinson Tree in the southern hemisphere.

According to the internet, this is where Donal lives.

Wilkinson Tree is another multi-owner tree, known as the San Francisco of Treetop, which is an insult to San Francisco. At least you can afford to live there on less than a million a year, now that Big Tech has mostly legged it to Arcadia, and I can't wait until Finian gets around to dealing with *that* nest of vipers. They've all got friends and relatives here, anyway. There's a university on one of the lower branches of Wilkinson Tree, and there are farmer's markets where you can buy produce from the local pond farms, and frozen yogurt stands everywhere.

Donal and Harriet have got a house on the Glades level, 5.5 miles up. At first I think I must have the wrong house because it's breathtakingly posh, three storeys with bamboo verandahs screened by curtains of moss. A colony of pretty little sunbirds twitters on the roof. Then I think I've *definitely* got the wrong house, because there are people trooping in and out as if it were a shop.

Attaching myself to the latest knot of visitors, I peek around a giant succulent moss and see Harriet holding court in a spacious living-room. She's wearing a caftan, kneeling on the polished wooden floor with a furry bundle on her lap. Women crowd around her. They stroke the bundle with shy fingers and coo adoringly.

The treecats have had kittens.

Is *that* how Donal and Harriet afforded this pile?

I knew the treecats would be popular as pets, if we could get a few tastemakers to adopt them. But the supply is limited, after all. I can't see treecats paying for this pile. Unless …

Dark suspicions float into my mind.

"Would you care for a mint julep?" says a feminine voice.

I reach for the offered drink, and jump out of my skin.

It's Ruby!

Before the burglary, he was living with us on Arcadia. He had to stop taking his stack of drugs, just like Imogen, when we ran out of money. He also had to go off the drugs he was on for his transition to female.

But after Kenneth and Vanessa, the other two members of our crew, stole the *Intergalactic Bogtrotter,* Ruby found a job at a black market biomodification clinic on Treetop's moon. It was a very dodgy place. Never mind transgender—most of the clients there were intending to become trans*species*. Ruby was working for drugs, basically. His transition is now complete. He's statuesque, with a glamorous wavy hairdo. The effect is somewhat spoiled by the maid's uniform he's got on.

His lipsticked mouth drops open. "Fletch? Everyone thought you were dead!"

"So did I, more than once. Jesus, Ruby, I thought *you* were dead."

"Obviously not, dude."

I shake my head. "How did you survive?"

When we last met, eight months ago, Ruby was piloting a security drone to cover our getaway from the Flower Lake Clinic. There was an extreme saleswoman with murderous intentions on our tail, and I've been worrying off and on that she and her associates may have taken it out on Ruby after we escaped their clutches.

"Where to start?" he says. "The NEPD shut down the clinic. And all the other clinics on the moon. There was a huge outcry, but maybe you know about that?"

"No."

"Society just isn't ready for extreme biomodification. It was a big defeat for the tech lobby, and a win for the NEPD. So, *not* an unmixed triumph for ordinary people. The NEPD are jackbooting around like they own the place."

I smirk, thinking about what the NEPD have in store for them when Finian reaches Earth.

"Donal and Harriet have been wonderful," Ruby says, smoothing his maid's uniform. "Absolutely wonderful."

"If you're not liking this gig, there's a place for you on Finian's crew."

"Finian?! Is he here?" Ruby looks around as if expecting him to jump out from behind a moss plant.

"He's around," I say vaguely. The whole galaxy will know Finian's precise whereabouts soon enough. "What about Donal?"

"He's on the third-floor verandah."

I find my way to the third-floor verandah without meeting anyone else I know. These people come from a different universe. They're stackers, or rich, or both. The only time they notice me is to frown at my jeans and Kyuss t-shirt ("The Wonder Wall shall now produce no clothing that isn't made of denim or leather or has a rock band's logo on it"—Finian's edict number 100-and-I-lost-count). Tibetan flute music wafts through the rooms on currents of perfectly chilled air.

Out on the verandah, the air conditioning doesn't work so well. The heat is overpowering and the sweet leaf scent coats my nostrils.

"A little of this place goes a long way, I'm finding," I say.

Donal falls out of his chair. He was only balanced on the edge of it, his upper body doubled over in the tense posture I remember from when things were going badly on the *Skint Idjit*. He was also smoking a cigarette, which he hasn't done in decades.

"Holy Mary, Mother of God," he says, picking himself up. He looks at his cigarette and stubs it out. Then he stares at me. "Is it really you, Fletch?"

"It is."

"Did no one offer you a drink?"

"Ruby did."

"If it was one of those julep things, I don't blame you. I think the caterers brought some Pepsi."

"I'm all right, lad."

"So … Jesus. Where have you been?"

I fill him in on the story of our adventures on the Ghost Train. I find myself skipping a lot of the important parts, such as Merrielande, and my attempt to vandalize the Tombs of Youth, and my headfirst dive down a Sagittarian toilet. Yes, there is a pattern here. I am skipping the parts where I come off as greedy, or desperate, or just plain stupid. Maybe sometime in the future I might feel comfortable enough to tell him the whole truth, and laugh at myself. But right now I don't feel like being entirely open with him.

Because he's obviously not been entirely open with me.

"So that's me," I finish. "What about yourself? You've come up in the world since we last met."

Donal leans back in his chair. He scrapes his blond hair back with both hands and lets it fall—a new nervous habit to add to his collection. The hair's grown out to his shoulders. He always had Adonis looks, but now he's added a bit of pudge, which he's trying to hide with loose linen trousers and a collarless blazer thing.

"I'm just trying to process it," he says. "The Ghost Train. A pocket universe inside the black hole at the center of the galaxy. A billion-year-old Sagittarian dictator …"

"Whose hobby was blowing up intelligent species to make sure he'd never have any competition. But we blew *him* away, so now the galaxy really is ours. Up humanity!"

"Aye, yeah. It's a bit much to take in."

"Every word of it's true."

That gets me a shocked look. "Jesus, Fletch, I'm not saying you're lying to me. We've known each other long enough."

But you *are* lying to me, Donal, I think, about something. We've known each other since we were five. I can tell.

I stand up, part the green curtain, and flinch from a shaft of baking sunlight. Out on the leaf in front of the house, giant yellow lilies fringe a pond. People sit in the shade of the lilies, working on portable computers. Frog-analogs croak. "It's a grand place you've got here," I say. "Did you pay off our backers at home all right?"

With what? That is what I want to know.

"Yeah. I refunded every last fiver." Suddenly he bursts out, "Ah God, I have to tell you. I'll understand if you're angry. You should be."

Here it comes. "Whatever it is, it doesn't matter. Go on."

"I kept the Gizmo. The treecats did their job perfectly, but the one I gave you was a fake. We swapped them on the catering plane. You went away with the fake one, and the real one stayed in Harriet's pocket. After you vanished, we auctioned it off."

I stare at him with my jaw on the floor.

I can't believe he did that to me.

After a minute, I shake my head, smiling in confusion. "It wasn't a fake, Donal. It worked fine, until the gandy dancers took it off us."

Now it's Donal's turn for his jaw to hit the floor.

"Ours was real," he insists. If it was a fake, the buyers would have come wanting their money back."

The verandah door rattles. "Both of them were real," Harriet says.

She steps out onto the verandah, barefoot, and goes to Donal. She sits on his knee. He winces.

"There were two Gizmos," she says, holding my eyes. "We trained the treecats to steal anything that looked like a five-inch nail. There were two. So they stole them both. I kept one for us and gave one to you. That's fair, isn't it?"

"But you said the one we gave Fletch was a fake." Donal's voice is hoarse with confusion.

"I wanted him out of our lives," Harriet says.

That's the hardest blow yet. I turn away from them, flapping my t-shirt away from my body. "Jesus it's hot."

The sunbirds twitter on the roof. The frogs croak in the lake. A treecat yowls within, and Harriet's friends laugh. The ceaseless rustle of leaves and creaking of boughs adds a layer of white noise to the soundscape, like city traffic.

A treecat nudges the door open and pads out onto the verandah. Harriet scoops it up and buries her face in its fur. When she looks up, her nose is pink and her eyes are wet. "Welcome home, Fletch, you asshole."

I'm willing to leave it at that. I don't want to sour things any further. Donal's got what he always wanted, even if it's the fruit of theft and deception. The best thing I can do for him now is to leave him be.

But he's shaking his head, getting angry. "You had no right to lie to me, Harry."

"She did the right thing," I say. "What've I ever brought you but trouble? The results speak for themselves. As soon as I'm out of the way, everything starts going right for you. I mean, look at this place. It's fecking amazing."

"I hate it," Donal says with quiet passion. "I thought I was going to love it here but I hate it."

Harriet's mouth falls open with surprise. She twists on his lap to face him. "You, too? Seriously?"

"You're joking, Harry! This is what you always wanted. I felt so bad about everything I've put you through. I wanted to give you the lifestyle you deserved."

"Maybe it is what I deserve," she says grimly. "The ultimate gated community with the ultimate trendy, superficially caring, oh-so-environmentally-pure neighbors. And God, those frogs! They never fucking shut up!"

"Now you know why I sleep with the pillow over my head," Donal says.

"And I thought it was because you didn't want me to hear you talking in your sleep," Harriet says. She turns to me. "He has nightmares about getting caught, Fletch. They don't suspect us. They think the Gizmo was stolen by that bio-modification gang that got rolled up last year. But he wakes up in the night kicking the sheets off, thinking they've come to put him in handcuffs."

Donal inhales noisily and meets my gaze. "Are you going to turn me in, Fletch?"

We're Irish. There is a lasting taboo against turning anyone in. The grass who squeals on his friends is the lowest form of life. This is the most insulting thing Donal's ever said to me.

I'm about to blow up at him when I see the look of humble resignation in his eyes. It hasn't even occurred to him that he's just insulted me. He's been away from Ireland so long that he's forgetting how to talk and think.

I nod slowly. "I suppose I'd better turn you in to the

NEPD. Put an end to your suffering."

Astonishment flashes in Donal's eyes. He never for a moment thought I really would squeal. I suppose that's good to know. But he masters his reaction, bows his head. "We deserve it."

"Oh no, we don't," Harriet says.

I speak over her. "Fortunately, the NEPD has a new chief. So I'll only be turning you in to Finian."

Yes, I left that part out when I told Donal my story. I thought I should wait to see how Finian's negotiations with Earth shake out. But I already know, don't I? Finian has the Ghost Train. That's all it will take for all the pols on Earth to crawl to him, offering him all the titles and baubles he wants, and it's fortunate for us that all he's ever wanted is to rove the galaxy, boozing and fighting. And there are plenty of pirates out there for him to fight.

I look at my watch. "In fact, he's on the local loop right now, but he'll be leaving in another hour. So we can still catch him if we step on it."

Donal lights up with a grin. He stands up, sliding Harriet off his lap, and kisses her. "I'll round up the treecats. You pack whatever you want to take."

"Nothing," she says. "I don't want to take anything. I just want to go home."

I smile. "You have got a car, have you? I don't want to take another taxi. They gouged me for two thousand dollars on the way here."

"We've got a new-model Mercedes-Benz 300SL."

"Grand. Then we're all set. Just bring your fiddle."

CHAPTER 17

So we sweep into orbit around Earth with a ceili in full swing in the lounge. Finian may be a diehard oldies fan, but he's also got a soft spot for the traditional songs. The Draconians also turn out to be musical souls. They can't sing but they make an amazing rhythm section. And most surprisingly of all, Owen Jones—Sam's longlost father—is a virtuoso on the pibgorn. What is a pibgorn? you ask. It is the Welsh version of the bagpipes. There's a kind of shuddering ache to the notes that makes even the Draconians lid their eyes. We're all the same under the skin.

Dear old Earth! Hardly have we glimpsed her cloud-garlanded majesty when military spaceships mob the Ghost Train. Targeting lasers dance over our hull. They never learn. All the same, I understand their reaction. The Ghost Train was not supposed to be back until 2068, and it has never stopped at Earth in the past. The politicians must be terrified.

Heh. They have no idea.

"Youse can get off now if you like," Finian says to us. "I'll deal with these wretches … Yeah, I fecking copy you.

Yeah, I am aware of that. Are you aware I've got nukes?" He chortles, leans back in the new captain's couch on the observation deck, and crackles his knuckles. "You have to start off by frightening them," he muses. "Then they learn."

I'm not sure, but I think this may be an oblique apology for the things he did to me in the past. If so, it's all right. I have learned.

"We'll be off, then, Finian."

We shake hands. The moment seems to last a long time.

"Say hello to your father for me. And don't forget my Guinness."

"I'll send you a whole brewery."

I have promised to ship him several cases of Guinness (cans being better than nothing), since the Wonder Wall still can't do carbonation.

Dizzy and Pew Pew meet us in the parking bay. They are supervising the construction of Finian's Formula One track. They wear jeans and heavy metal t-shirts now. They look extremely cute. "DO YOU WISH TO TAKE FLYING SAUCER?" Dizzy suggests hopefully. "I WOULD LIKE TO SEE FACES OF HUMANS WHEN YOU LAND ON WHITE HOUSE LAWN."

Sometimes I'm *sure* the gandy dancers are more autonomous than they let on.

"Jesus, we're not going to the White House," I say.

"We are," Sam grins.

He has a whole elaborate scheme to meet the President of the United States and 'help' them negotiate with Finian, by which he means trousering big bucks as a consultant. Despite all we've been through, he is still quite naïve in some ways.

"We are not going to the bloody White House," says Owen Jones, in his gravelly voice. "We are going to the maximum security international prison in the Seychelles to see your mother. We're taking this." He holds up a Gizmo cut from one of the Tombs of Youth. Finian hacked it off for them himself.

Sam hesitates. "I'm afraid we're gonna be too late," he says in a nearly inaudible voice.

"It is never too late to make amends," Owen Jones says. "We'll take the Denebite star shuttle. That is, if you don't mind, Fletch."

"No, you're fine," I say. "We'll just take the police cruiser."

So, with Imogen at the wheel, we deorbit from Earth's local loop and skid down through the atmosphere …

In over the Pacific …

Across North America …

The treecats yowl in the boot.

Across the Atlantic …

… and down, down, down to the raggedy-edged blot of land west of Britain.

Ireland is swathed in damp gray clouds. It's winter. I'd forgotten about that. Forgotten about the seasons.

Imogen's cut the engines by now. We're coasting on anti-grav. We still come in fast enough to terrify the cows in Mahoney's top field. I roll down my window, gulping in the damp sea-tinged air, as we skim over the hedge, touch down, jolt forward—and bury the nose in another hedge.

Auld Mahoney bursts out of his back door, cellphone in hand.

I leap out one side of the police cruiser. Donal leaps out

the other. "Mr Mahoney! Don't call the guards! It's us!"

I have uttered these words, or ones like them, all too often. Hopefully that will change now.

We get away with minimal damage after Donal talks the auld fella into accepting an IOU in compensation for the 'stress' we have caused his prizewinning Jerseys. Then it's off across the fields to my house, which is closer. Harriet and Imogen both complain about the wet grass, the wind, and the 'scary' sheep we meet on the lane. Harriet, ebullient, laughs at herself for being such a city girl. She's going to like it here, I think. Not Imogen. She just goes quiet.

"Da?"

I don't bother knocking on the back door. I just ease it open.

"Mum?"

"Jesus Mary and Joseph, ALLAN IT'S FLETCH, oh Jesus Christ come here and let me hug you, my little boy …"

I love my mother.

My father comes out of the sitting-room, where the television is going full blast. "I was just watching Finian on the telly, bellowing on in his old style about the oppression of the little guy and how that's got to end, thinking to myself Jesus, that really is my brother … and now here's you."

He doesn't look much like Finian, my dad. He's just as tall, but thinner, like me, his ranginess turning to boniness now in his old age. Also unlike Finian, Dad is softspoken and courteous, as befits a professor of systems design.

"And Donal O'Leary! You two have been on your travels. And I see you've brought back the greatest treasure of all: a pair of lovely ladies."

Harriet smiles—she loves that kind of thing. Imogen,

prickly, says with a grimace, "Female human being will do, thanks."

As my mother's putting the kettle on, Dad draws me out the back door on the pretext of showing me the logs he's got in for the winter, which he wants me to chop. Wood stoves are all the rage now that we've not got to worry about CO_2 anymore. Thank you, A-tech carbon sequestration. "Is that bird of yours a stacker?" my father asks.

He's amazing the way he can always tell. But it's because he works with so many of them. As the years go on, stackers are taking over the top levels of all the brainwork professions. Understandably, as a professor, Dad's got a bit of a chip on his shoulder about that. There's more than one kind of intelligence, he's always said. There's more to people than what you can measure.

"She is, Da, yeah."

"I see."

"Don't worry, I don't think she'll be sticking around long."

When we go back in, the tea is ready. We all sit around the kitchen table with mugs of tea and a plate of Jaffa cakes, as well as slices of my mother's barm brack.

My prediction about Imogen comes true within just a few moments. After one bite of barm brack, she gets up to leave, saying she is worried about the police cruiser. She wants to make sure she can get home to Canada in it.

I follow her out the back door. "Can you find your way all right?"

"I'm sure I can figure it out," she says, flinching away from Mum's chickens, which live in the old byre where my childhood BMX bike is still rusting.

We walk together down the lane. I wish she'd come when the fuschias were in bloom. It's a bit grim at this time of year. But I love it anyway. This little patch of planet Earth is more beautiful than any alien planet. The damp air, the dead cow parsley in the verges, the wagtails hopping on the grass down the middle of the lane—every little tiny thing is precious. Priceless.

We go through the gate into our bottom field, which is a mass of weeds since my family hasn't farmed in generations, and slog up through two more fields to the top of the hill. We left the cruiser on the far side of here.

Licheny boulders bulge from the sheep-cropped grass. The wind sweeps over the hilltop, carrying sheets of misty-moisty drizzle. "Come up here," I urge Imogen, balancing on the highest rock. "You can see the steeple of Lisdoonvarna church. You'd be able to see the sea from here, too, if the weather was better."

"It's *raining*," she says pitifully.

"It's just a drizzle."

"I need to get back to the cruiser. I don't want a parking ticket."

"You won't get a parking ticket in auld Mahoney's field."

"I don't even know if I've got enough juice to reach Canada. I might have to stop in London or somewhere."

As my father says, there's more than one kind of intelligence.

And more than one kind of stupidity.

"Anyway. Bye, Fletch."

Imogen plods down the hill, her back stooped, her head bare to the drizzle.

Suddenly she stops and lets out a shriek.

I fly down the hill to her. "What is it? Jesus, Imogen, what's wrong?"

Her mouth wobbles. Tears spill from her eyes. "I stepped in cow poop," she wails.

I manage not to laugh. Impulsively, I take her in my arms. Her arms go around my neck, clinging.

And I kiss her, soft and long, never giving a damn that I'm stepping in the offending cowpat, too.

When we get back to my house, everyone's on their second cup of tea, the treecats are rampaging under the table, and Harriet is telling my parents how grim Treetop is. "Don't believe everything you read on the gossip sites."

Donal grins openly to see me and Imogen hand in hand.

"I decided to stay for a while," Imogen says. She sits down beside me and picks up her abandoned slice of barm brack. She chews thoughtfully, and then her eyes widen. She says to my mother, "Nuala, this is incredible!"

"It's just home cooking," my mother smiles.

"I guess it's been a while since I was … home."

"Consider this your home," says Mum. "For as long as you need."

Did I mention I love my mother?

Dad's still looking a bit sour. He watches the treecats climbing the curtains. "Is that all you brought back?" he says. "You were going to come back rich beyond the wildest dreams, etcetera."

Donal grins. "Allan, I *am* rich beyond my wildest dreams." He slides his arm around Harriet's waist. "This is the only treasure I need."

"Aaaah," says my mother. She's a romantic. I get it from her.

"Besides," Donal says, turning practical, "we're going to make a mint breeding treecats. I'm thinking we'll buy the old Healy farm on the coast road, if it's still on the market, and turn the milking shed into a cattery."

My father shakes his head. "They're grand wee beasts. But what about all the A-tech you were going to find? What happened to that?"

"A-tech," I say, "is overrated."

I was going to save this for later. But I'm so happy that I can't hold it back.

"I've brought back something better."

"Is that it?" Dad says, nodding at the lightsaber stuck in my cargo pocket. "I thought that was the thing you pinched off Finian when you were twenty."

"It's a different one, but no, that's not it."

I put down my tea mug and reach into my back pocket. When I've got everyone's attention, I unfold a sheet of material that looks like paper but isn't. It comes out almost the size of the kitchen table.

On it is printed a snarl of lines, festooned with notations, all superimposed on a spiral whorl.

"Even Finian hasn't got one of these," I say.

I can say this with confidence, because I searched all over the Ghost Train to make sure there was not a duplicate somewhere. I even asked the gandy dancers. They offered to buy this one off me. Not a chance.

"But what is it?" says my mother.

"I snatched it off the noticeboard at the Nursing Home in the Core of the Galaxy. It's a map—"

"—of the entire Interstellar Railroad," Donal finishes for me, laughing in delight. "It's priceless!" There's not a shred of bitterness in that man. "Well done, Fletch!"

Imogen stares, rapt, at the map. "We could sell this for billions."

"We could."

"Or we could go and explore the far side of the galaxy."

I groan. "We could."

"Or we could put it up on the internet, for everyone to use, and do something else."

"Like what?" I have a fair idea what she's going to say. We talked about it on the way back from the hill, before she knew about the map.

"Well, you have some fields out there that are just going to waste. This used to be a farm, didn't it?"

My father says uneasily, "I don't know the first thing about cows."

I hug him. "Don't worry, Dad. It's in the genes. We'll figure it out."

This is the conclusion of Fletcher Connolly's (mostly unwanted) adventures on the Interstellar Railroad.

DISCOVER THE ADVENTUROUS WORLDS
OF FELIX R. SAVAGE

An exuberant storyteller with a demented imagination, Felix R. Savage specializes in creating worlds so exciting, you'll never want to leave.

Join the Savage Stories newsletter to get notified of new releases and chances to win free books:

www.felixrsavage.com/signup

THE SOL SYSTEM RENEGADES SERIES

Near-Future Hard Science Fiction

A genocidal AI is devouring our solar system. Can a few brave men and women save humanity?

In the year 2288, humanity stands at a crossroads between space colonization and extinction. Packed with excitement, heartbreak, and unforgettable characters, the Sol System Renegades series tells a sweeping tale of struggle and deliverance.

Crapkiller
The Galapagos Incident
The Vesta Conspiracy
The Mercury Rebellion
The Luna Deception
The Phobos Maneuver
The Mars Shock
The Callisto Gambit

Keep Off The Grass (short story)
A Very Merry Zero-Gravity Christmas (short story)

THE RELUCTANT ADVENTURES
OF
FLETCHER CONNOLLY
ON THE
INTERSTELLAR RAILROAD

Near-Future Non-Hard Science Fiction

An Irishman in space. Untold hoards of alien technological relics waiting to be discovered. What could possibly go wrong?

Skint Idjit
Intergalactic Bogtrotter
Banjaxed Ceili
Supermassive Blackguard

FIRST CONTACT, INC.

Not A User's Manual

The alien rulers of the galaxy are pyramid marketers, and humanity's role in the grand scam is to play the sucker at the bottom.

Unless we can find suckers of our own to prey on ...

Against The Rules
Payback

COMING SOON ...

ESCAPE BURN

Very-Near-Future Very Hard Science Fiction

NASA isn't telling you what the Juno probe really found.

The discovery of an apparently wrecked alien spacecraft in orbit around Europa sparks a massive, multinational effort to build a spaceship capable of reaching Jupiter with present-day technology. But overcoming technical and political hurdles will be just the beginning of a terrifying journey for pilot Jack Kildare and seven other astronauts. Their unprecedented voyage into deep space will alter humanity's future forever ... *if they survive.*

Ship One
Burn Two
Planet Three

15135115R00090

Printed in Poland
by Amazon Fulfillment
Poland Sp. z o.o., Wrocław